Thirteen Plus-1
Lovecraftian Narratives

Thirteen Plus-1

Lovecraftian Narratives

Nancy Kilpatrick

Foreword by S. T. Joshi

eBook: ISBN 978-1-9992600-4-0
Print: ISBN 978-1-9992600-5-7

Author's Note: Many people over time bring an author to a collection of stories. Specific to this collection, I want to thank Lovecraftian scholar S. T. Joshi for his overall kindness and help in making this book a reality. He has always been supportive of my work and for a writer, that is gold! Joshi and David E. Schultz formatted this book out of the kindness of their hearts. Caro Soles proofed my work with her lovely, intelligent, critical eye. And I will be forever in debt to Istvan Kadar who has created my most beautiful and interesting book covers, including this one. Istvan, you are a genius! I am grateful to you, my readers, for your trust in choosing this volume. Ultimately, these stories would not exist without the ingenious mind of H. P. Lovecraft, whose oeuvre paved the foundation for most writers of weird fiction, including me.

—Nancy Kilpatrick 2023

Contents

Foreword

There was a time when writing pastiches of the work of H. P. Lovecraft was the literary equivalent of slumming. Authors of such tales seemed to be content with adding a new "god" or "forbidden book" to Lovecraft's open-ended pseudomythology, and these works—even when written by professional writers—were for the most part not much better than "fan fiction." Even the most prominent writer of these stories, August Derleth (Lovecraft's friend and publisher, who bestowed the name Cthulhu Mythos to Lovecraft's creation), demonstrated repeatedly that he fundamentally misunderstood the whole nature and purpose of Lovecraft's literary output.

But in the last several decades things have changed radically. It has now became evident that Lovecraft's signature contribution to weird fiction is "cosmicism"—the depiction of the spatial and temporal vastness of the universe and the inconsequence of the human race within those realms. Such writers as Ramsey Campbell, T. E. D. Klein, Thomas Ligotti, Caitlín R. Kiernan, and Jonathan Thomas used Lovecraft's mythos as a springboard for their own views on humanity's relations to the cosmos. And now Nancy Kilpatrick has joined their number.

Nancy was a veteran writer of the weird well before she ventured into Lovecraftian fiction. Although the earliest of the stories in this book dates to 1995, Nancy has been publishing professionally since the late 1980s. It has been my privilege to solicit contributions from her for my own Lovecraftian anthologies over the past decade or more. I could always count on her to deliver a work that pays homage to the fundamentals of the Lovecraftian ethos while also expressing her own provocative thoughts on the tenuous status of human beings in an incomprehensible universe.

In these fourteen tales, set in an evocatively rendered contemporary world and filled with characters enlivened by her sensitivity to the finest shades of fluctuating emotion, Nancy has generated an existential horror in a manner that Lovecraft chose to avoid. His writing—by turns scientifically austere and poetically flamboyant—took little interest in the human characters he put on stage; for him, these were simply the eyes, ears, and mind of readers as they became enmeshed in the bizarre. For Nancy, the human characters are always troubled by the angst unique to our own unsettled age, and yet she can also generate cosmic terror reminiscent of the greatest of Lovecraft's own narratives.

Nancy Kilpatrick is a renowned and accomplished writer who has demonstrated mastery of all the many modes and phases of weird fiction. In these tales she takes on a giant of twentieth-century horror and proves that she can express terror and dread in ways that even Lovecraft could not. But amidst the fear you will sense in these brooding narratives, you will also be enriched by an awareness of the many unnerving aspects of our life in this new century.

—S. T. JOSHI

A Crazy Mistake

When I began this research, I had no intention of travelling down such a dark and horrifying path. In fact, I was in a relatively good frame of mind, enjoying myself in the mildly cynical howbeit jovial manner I once was known for. I had work and all was right with my little world. At least for a while.

Bottom line—and I have to remember this—I'm just a low-level researcher, someone who scans history, mythology and legend to find interesting bits that movie directors can use in their science fiction, fantasy and horror films. I'm the person responsible for discovering ancient lore about such stock supernaturals as vampires, werewolves, elves, ghosts, dragons, UFOs and zombies, and digging out factoids from the collective fantasies of the past that can be spun into something fresh and modern yet still recognizable for a ninety-minute screen-scream aimed mainly at fraternities sharing a kegger with sororities, both cliques hoping to get lucky, cine-grisly playing as romantic background noise.

I have no illusions. My work will never win me a Nobel prize. I'll never even win one of the Oscars you *don't* see on television that are given behind the scenes because nobody cares about the researcher or research team. My work is silly, pointless in a way. It's a job, one I try to enjoy, that pays well, and probably keeps me from losing my mind. Or, I *used* to enjoy it.

This madness that's engulfing me now began when I was asked to research early religions for a Tarantino-imitation split story about mummies and space creatures to see if anything in the oldest spirituality humans adopted could be spun into a somewhat believable yarn as back tale for an apocalyptic invasion-from-space film that features desiccated insectoids and half-naked women. "We're an alien experiment," the director chirped excitedly, philosophizing from his near-constant inebriated state. At the best of times, he tends to present ideas that have been headlining tabloids and floating through the Internet forever as if he invented them. "Aliens are big, Kim. Everybody believes they were here before us and have been for a long time. See if you can find the first women they knocked up. You know, the Amazons or something."

My initial reaction should have been: *Kevin, lay off the small-c: coke!* But of course, I said nothing like that. This work is my bread and butter. And with the young and restless clawing at my heels, I'm finding myself not as in-demand as I once was. Hence, my personal script has become stock phrases, something along the lines of: "Yeah, Kev, I know exactly where you're coming from. I'm sure I can find something you can use."

And so it went. I had the fat contract and the usual two weeks to find back story material for what would ultimately be labeled a low-budget waste-of-time turkey that goes straight to Blu-ray and on Netflix and Amazon B-movies list.

The day I began the research, I realized I had a huge problem on my hands. A quick search on the Net brought up very little but I did find that not much had been written about the early religions and the women who espoused them, at least not in the easily digestible bytes found virtually. In fact, it seemed humans only started chiseling the details in stone when the patriarchal-religion guys took charge.

"So, Franklin," I asked when I phoned my high-school

best-buddy, college boyfriend, now lifelong-friend who is working on his third MA, this one in comparative religions at Miskatonic University in New England, "this is more complicated than I thought."

"Kim, you have no idea. I don't even go there. My area of study is the patriarchal religions. Some people don't even believe there were matriarchies."

"Do you?"

A typical Franklin pause, followed by a decidedly oblique answer. "Occasionally an anthropologist will attribute a certain significance to *objet d'art* in matrifocality without applying undue emphasis on female power-rule——"

"In English."

"There are social scientists who believe that some prehistory societies *might* have had women as heads of the society, but the notion of them as power-oriented hasn't been proven."

"Okay, so they did exist. And you kind of agree that they did, right? A yes or no answer, please."

"A qualified yes."

"What about the Amazons?"

"What about them?"

"Well, they were female rule, right?"

"They were warriors during the classical antiquity— around the time of ancient Greece. There's plenty of information about the Amazons, much of it mythology. But I thought you were looking for early religions."

"Well, kind of. What do you know about the Amazons?"

And he told me of virgin warrioresses pre-Xena who wouldn't have anything to do with men until they wanted to breed female children, who cut off their left breasts so they could more easily use a bow and arrow or a spear, who were big and tall and strong and could fight the male of the species the way Kate Beckinsale takes on macho Lycans.

"They've even got their own commemorative genre of art—amazonomoachy."

After a ten-minute lecture, I figured I had enough information that Kev would be thrilled. Especially the virgin part. He seemed to have a penchant for virgins.

Still, I wanted to do a thorough job. Despite being a research hack, I'd always held to a few standards I tried to maintain, just so I could look myself in the mirror the morning after the movie premiered.

"So, I can get a book on the Amazons?"

"Easily. Look in the classical mythology section of the library, or, better yet, buy a couple of comic books."

"Snide comments will be overlooked, my friend."

A Franklin-style guffaw.

"What about the pre-historic matriarchies? Where can I get facts about them."

"Nowhere."

"Well, if they existed——"

"They're *assumed* to have existed from the pottery and clay figures left behind that predate recorded history."

"There's nothing written about them?"

"There are a few books that postulate their existence, based on these finds, and also looking at what we know about early female-based goddess worshipping cultures usurped by aggressive northern patriarchal cultures and their religions conquering, if you will, of the more feminine-based societies and changing the notion of deitification by 2,400 B.C.E. For example, the Mesopotamians—a patriarchal culture with male deities invaded Egypt around 3,000 B.C.E. From what we can ascertain, prior to that time, goddesses in goddess-based religions ruled alone, most of the time their son as their lover——"

"Ick!"

"—and gradually through the influence of the patriarchal

societies that conquered, over time that young male figure ascended to power while the female's power declined. That took place in the day to day lives of ancient Egyptians too, where the line was previously mother-kinship, going through the females, and women transacted business while men were occupied with weaving and other artistic endeavors. But regarding the gods, we know, for instance, that in ancient Egypt the female deity Au Set—Isis to you and most people—had a son or brother consort, Osiris. By 3,000 B.C.E. Osiris had risen to ruler with Isis identified as his sister who he married. So, voila, her position was more or less usurped!"

"Yeah. The glass ceiling of the goddesses. Anyway, what books?"

He gave me a list of a dozen volumes, starting with one published in 1861. Johann Jakob Bachofen authored *Mother Right: An Investigation of the Religious and Juridical Character of Matriarchy in the Ancient World*. "It's the bible," he said.

Although Bachofen's book had a fair following over the next few generations, Franklin assured me I probably wouldn't find it for sale. "It's long out of print, even the modern reprintings, but you might find a used copy if you do a search and you can surely track it down in the stacks of a university reference library."

"Which would mean a trip back to the east coast to see you if I had more than two weeks, which I don't."

"Worry not, Kim, I'm busy as the proverbial bee. It isn't that I wouldn't love to hang out with you too, but even if you had a month, I'm jammed up with seminars and I'm in the middle of writing my thesis. This phone call is about all the time I can spare."

"Oh," I said a bit grumpily. "Well, I guess I can save the airfare!"

"Don't be petulant. It doesn't become you. And you know

I'd see you in a New York minute if I could."

"I know. I'm sorry, Franklin. Sometimes I just miss the old days a lot. I miss you."

Another pause, this one his now-what-do-I-say? hesitation. I'm the one who broke it off; I felt I had to. I'd sculpted him into more father figure and less lover and I could see I was suffocating him with my unspoken demands that he be the parent that had abandoned my mother and me when I was a child. He had to focus on school. I understood that—at least intellectually. Emotionally, I felt deserted.

One day I had packed a suitcase and moved to LA. I got work in the film business, spending my days and nights contributing to the cesspool of cheap B-and-lesser-grade movies for the entertainment of the lowest common denominator, which career move effectively buried my feelings. Franklin's the one who carried the torch for a long time. Despite that, he forgave me, eventually, and we've been best friends since.

"So, those books?" I reminded him. "On matriarchies? What *can* I get my hands on easily."

"Yeah," he said, his voice a little strained. But he was on familiar turf again and quickly directed me to two specific volumes on the list.

Modern research began with Bachofen but the newer titles—mainly by women, most written when feminism was first gaining ground in the 1970s—were scholarly enough that likely they had based their good research on using the older tomes, saving me the time and energy. I called around and found *When God Was a Woman* by Merlin Stone at a women's book store in Berkley and had them ship to SoCa via overnight.

"We're good?" I asked, as I'd ended my conversation with Franklin.

"Always, Kim."

"Let's try to get together when you have a break from

classes, maybe in the summer."

"I'd like that. But listen, if you hit a snag, call me. I didn't mean to sound unavailable to you."

"I know. Me too with you."

The book turned out to be a hard slog for me. Never of an academic bent, the various names of early female deities and the names of ancient societies began to blur quickly in my mind. Where was Samarra again? Who was this worshiped goddess named Astarte, aka Inanna, Nut, Anahita, Istar, Attoret, Hathor and a dozen other names, revered throughout the Middle East in the past? The author traced some of these deities back to carvings from the Neolithic era, 7000 B.C.E., and some even as far back as 25,000 B.C.E. and the upper Palaeolithic cultures, and a bit of this early artwork was still extant. These were the figures Franklin told me about, one or two of which I'd seen on the Net, and which I was now viewing photographs of in the book, everything from anorexic stick figures to images which looked as if they needed stomach stapling by today's standards.

They were fairly similar but for the oldest one, from 25,000 B.C.E. Try as I might to make sense of this grossly obese figure with what appeared to be a beehive—not her hairdo, but on her head—I could not. The author described it as an Upper Palaeolithic *Venus* figure, one of several found throughout Europe and Asia from the same period. The only other image that came vaguely close was one from Anatolia dating much later, 5750 B.C.E. But the heads of those earliest-found Venus figures did not resemble anything human to me, and I couldn't see a connection to the 3rd century B.C.E. Roman goddess of love and beauty and the exquisite images of her that still exist.

I put the book down. Maybe Palaeolithic humans made no connection between what they saw and what they sculpted in clay. But did that seem reasonable? The earliest of the 350 prehistoric cave paintings discovered was radio-carbon dated from 37,000 B.C.E. and the animals—99.9 percent of what our ancestors depicted—looked very much like animals that we see today. Still, 12,000 years later, shouldn't artistry have evolved? Why would this later 'Venus figure' with a real beehive be so strangely distorted?

Goddess worship, as the books defined the matriarchal spiritual beliefs, was a natural view back then based on the flesh and blood women who existed. Before fecundity and co-itus were understood as leading to childbirth, women were seen as the source of life since only they could give birth and the input of males wasn't yet known. Also, women were the main source of food production, so they sustained life too.

Despite my lack of academic acumen, I soon became obsessed with pre-historic goddess-worshiping societies and resolved to try to find out more, particularly about the oldest, weirdest images.

I kept the movie research to the Amazons and Kev was thrilled with just knowing, "They were virgins! Yeah, that's good, Kim, real good. I can use that."

The check arrived and was duly cashed and it allowed me to take some time off work. Standing in line at the bank, a brilliant idea struck: I could spend a few days researching matriarchies! It would be like a mini vacation. And despite Franklin's warning to not bother him, I caught a flight east, heading directly to Miskatonic U's vast research library. I had access to the library through Franklin, when I was still his significant other, and neither of us saw much reason to change overlapping library cards and insurance policies. I didn't tell him I was coming though, but he somehow found out and tracked me down in the stacks.

"Kim, what are you doing here? And why didn't you let me know?"

"You're busy. I didn't want to disturb you," I said, staring sheepishly up at his so-open rosy-cheeked face. I'd always loved his sandy hair and eyes—I found them as restful as sandstone sculptures, especially so now after two weeks of *not* seeing the sun while immersing myself in tomes that weighed more than me.

"For god's sake, Kim, I'm not *that* busy we couldn't meet for dinner or something," he said, shaking his head at me in that way that always made me laugh.

But then he just stared at me the way a doctor examines a patient. "You look pale. And you've lost weight. Are you sick?"

"No. A little tired maybe——"

"You look like you haven't eaten in days. Come on. I'm buying dinner."

"An offer I can't refuse," I said.

He watched me place the book that I was about to reread onto the librarian's cart.

He tilted his head and read aloud: *"The Great Old Ones.* What's that about, Kim?"

"I'll tell you over supper."

We ate at the student cafeteria. He had meatloaf—he always had meatloaf when it was available. I was still a vegetarian and ordered a plate of vegetables-of-the-day but felt too agitated to do more than pick at the food.

"Franklin, that book?"

"The one I saw?"

"Yeah. It's from the mythology section. The story of how life on earth began."

"There is no shortage of theories," he said, stuffing his mouth with gravy-soaked mashed potatoes.

"This one's pretty bizarre. It talks about extraterrestrials—those are the Great Old Ones. They arrived long before there was anything on this planet. Or maybe when there was some life. There are several myths."

"No shortage of mythos either."

"In fact, they're the ones who created life."

"A creation mythology."

"Kind of. But, it's different. I mean, you know about religions, right? Why did God create humans?"

"Lots of theories there too. As many as there are religions."

"Give me some examples."

"Are you going to eat your peas?"

"No." I shoved my plate towards him and he scooped up teaspoons of grey-green canned peas, then stared lustfully at my carrot coins.

"Well, with Judeo-Christian it's man-in-His-own-image—that's a classic. The Hindu god Brahma is said to have created the universe, with some help—they don't know why but the general feeling is that everybody had the best of intentions. The Muslim's believe that Allah is manifesting his might and will through us as conscious beings so that we will know and love Him, and one another. The Buddhists say the beginning of this world is inconceivable, no beginning, no end, no reason. The matriarchies you were so hot about a few weeks ago, it seems they made a connection between the cycles of birth, life, death, rebirth, and the birth of the universe——"

"Okay, but none of this sounds bad."

He stopped chewing and thought about it. "No, I guess not. It's all good."

"But what about a religion that believes their God or Gods just, I don't know, made life, but it was a mistake."

"That's pretty far out, Kim."

"This book, *The Great Old Ones*, that's exactly what it suggests. That there were these aliens that have always existed and they just go around doing things without any real intent. Well, maybe there's an intent to have fun, like play practical jokes on each other, or play games, maybe malicious. And sometimes they do something and it's a mistake. Like making us. We're a mistake. Or a nasty joke. But they don't really care."

"That doesn't sound like any religion I've studied."

"I know. This is so weird. They didn't create us for any *good* reason. And you know what else, Franklin? The book, it refers to an expedition from the 1930s that started out at this very university——"

"From Miskatonic?"

"—and they discovered remains. Some scientists from here went to Antarctica and they found these gods, or maybe creatures they created. They might have found the Great Old Ones!"

Franklin put down his fork and eyed me the way people stare at a woman who might be losing her mind. "Okay, Kim, you're going off the deep end with this."

"What I'm *going* to do is ferret out more information about these Great Old Ones! I want to know about why they created life!"

"Look, come to my place. We'll have some wine and relax and you can tell me more about all this," he said.

The library was closed and I thought maybe relaxing wasn't such a bad idea. I *was* tired, physically and mentally. "All right, but I need to be at the library when it opens. I don't want anyone else getting to that book before I do!"

As we exited the cafeteria, Franklin said, "Kim, do you think that's likely, an esoteric volume like that?"

"You never know who is interested in what, Franklin. The more I investigate this, the more I feel I'm on the edge of a breakthrough."

"Just so it isn't a breakdown," he said in a soft voice, then draped his arm around my shoulder, just like the old days.

I spent more weeks in the library, rereading everything they had on matriarchies, including the Bachofen book, and the scant info available on these *Great Old Ones*. The librarian told me there were only two other volumes that even mentioned them, both focusing on the 1930s expedition. One was a scholarly assessment of the research materials gathered, saddled with the language of academia, littered with dry facts, devoid of any emotional response, an overwritten account of the fossils collected in the Antarctica expedition which were laboriously identified and classified by their Greek and Latin names, and none of which appeared to be remains of anything unidentifiable. I found the 300-page report migraine-inducing and with only one reference to Elder Gods. In the end it proved useless for my purposes.

The other book, though, a slim volume, was hand-written, an account by one of the explorers who didn't identify himself and wrote in the third person. Besides over thirty assistants and aircraft mechanics and the fifty-five sled dogs brought along, the heavy-hitters scientifically included a biologist, a geologist, a physicist/meteorologist and an engineer. This strange little book, scrawled on the yellowing parchment-like pages of a notebook of the day, had no title and the librarian had handed it over the desk reluctantly, insisting that I had to sit at the study table right in front of her, and reminding me to keep the protective gloves *on* and "Don't crease the pages!"

According to the anonymous author, the expedition used a newly-invented drill to sever ice as they moved to various geologically-significant spots on the continent, mainly south of the Ross Sea.

They had set sail from Boston Harbor on September 2, 1930 and reached the Antarctic Circle on October 20th, returning home by mid-February of the following year. The party landed on Ross Island and proceeded from there by dogsled interspersed with airplane flights to locations far-ther afield.

When one of their little planes was forced to land by bad weather, some of these intrepid explorers accidently discov-ered a previously unknown mountain range that rivaled the Himalayas. And then, they found a cave. And then they found the remains.

I reread the description of the remains: *bulbous things, with gills and wings, barrel bodies, suction cups at the end of multiple proboscis. Animals, likely marine, but maybe not. Anon identified them as 'Elder Things' and likened them to the 'Great Old Ones' of some religious mythology I didn't know about, with five-lobed brains. There was also a com-parison to bees!*

I put down the book, making the instant connection to the beehive-headed goddess figure. And a shiver ran through me. I felt at the edge of insight but I wasn't there yet, and read on.

The main body of the expedition lost radio contact with the smaller party that had discovered these remains. Con-sequently, some from the base camp were forced to hunt for their now-silent companions who would, ultimately, be found dead. And that's when they discovered what appeared to be the ruins of a city. A city built for gargantuans. The writer described it in one paragraph as constructed like *the cells of a honeycomb!*

I felt rattled to my bones. Surely this couldn't be con-nected to the matriarchal clay figures from 25,000 B.C.E.!

This is when it all turned very weird for me because at that point, the narrative stopped—the rest of the pages of the notebook had been ripped out. I counted remnants in the binding and it looked like the last third of the account was missing. I was a little afraid the librarian would blame me for this destruction so I turned to her and said, "Do you know that some of the pages of this book are missing?"

"Yes," she told me, "that's why you have to sit here and read it. Someone tore out the pages. It's an invaluable, historical account and we need to protect what remains."

I nodded at her and turned back to the notebook. Someone didn't want the rest of this story told!

As I'd read through the notebook, I noticed sketches the author had made of art on the walls of this giant city. I'd only given them a cursory look so I could keep reading the difficult-to-decipher script. But now I went back to them and studied what appeared to me to be almost a story in images, a bizarre history of some prehistoric race. As I examined each page of drawings, for some reason, those on page thirteen held my interest. That page contained images of what I would call *creatures*, something like animals, but not exactly animals. There were recognizable features: beaks and tentacles and multi-leggeds, the familiar stuck onto grotesque shapes, monstrous really, that sent another chill along my spine. And then, at the bottom right corner, I saw one figure with an enormous human body, a female, but not the head—the head was a beehive!

A small scream came from me and the librarian instantly shushed me.

"Kim, what's up?"

I looked up to see Franklin standing there. From the look on his face, I knew my face reflected the horror I felt.

"What is it?" his voice was full of concern as he sat next to me and put a hand on my shoulder.

I turned the notebook and showed him the picture. "Peculiar," he said. "Kind of fantastical drawings. When were they done?"

"In the 1930s."

"Strange images." He looked at me. "Reminds me of early

science fiction creatures. But why do you find them so up-setting?"

"Don't you see it, Franklin? Look. Look!"

The librarian hissed, "You'll have to keep your voice down!"

I whispered to Franklin rapidly as I frantically pointed to the image, "The huge woman with the beehive-head!"

He looked again. "Yeah, I see a resemblance, but——"

"This is the *same* image as the oldest matriarchal clay figure! I'm sure of it! They're identical!"

He stared at me. "Well, maybe it's similar, but——"

"No, it's the same! It's *exactly* the same!"

My voice must have risen again because the librarian was suddenly at my side, taking the book from my hands and saying, "I'm afraid I'll have to ask you to leave. You're disturbing others. And we must protect our books——"

"No!" I yelled, grabbing the notebook, almost snatching it back from her grasp.

"Kim, don't do that!" Franklin grabbed my arm.

As I pulled the book, the librarian held on tight and suddenly the fragile notebook broke apart, half in her hands, half in mine.

"Kim! What are you doing?"

The librarian called over her shoulder to a colleague, "Betty, call security, now!"

"Franklin, it's the same. It *is!* The Great Old Ones. They *did* start life here. They made the first women, but they made them wrong, they're not like us but they are, the same bodies, but not the heads. Not the heads! They made them like that as a joke!"

I don't recall much after that, other than being in a speeding ambulance, Franklin sitting pensively beside me, holding my hand, the sound of the siren loud in my ears, and someone in a uniform that looked medical injecting fluid into a vein on the back of my hand.

It took weeks for the psychiatrist at the university-affil-iated hospital to convince me, through drugs and psycho-therapy, that I'd been making connection that just were not there. "Sometimes, Kim, it appears to make sense to put things together that don't go together, and then it becomes easy to let an idea of a connection form. We all do that from time to time. It's mis-thinking. It's a way to simplify what in reality is too large a concept to understand. For instance, in this case, how life on earth began. Even the greatest scien-tific minds on the planet don't know the answer to that one. It's a mystery . . ."

Franklin visited me every day. He assured me I was overstressed, overworked, that I'd gotten myself in too deeply with academic research and that really wasn't my forte. He told me that you can't always put one and one to-gether and make two, which I didn't really understand, but I did appreciate his kindness and sweetness and suddenly saw that the loyal man I'd run away from in fear of destroy-ing both of us was the one I desperately wanted to walk to-wards. But I knew I could not do that. Not now. Not with what I knew. I'd completely destroy him.

When the hospital released me, Franklin insisted I move in with him. He's busy with his thesis and I know he doesn't want distractions so I try to keep out of his way. I'll stay here temporarily and try to recoup whatever sanity I have left. I'll make an effort to build a new life, one that allows me to act as if this great horror that overwhelms me is not real.

The library didn't press charges because they got the notebook back and I guess were able to repair the damage. Most of it, anyway. All but the bottom right corner of the sketch on page thirteen. That's the part I managed to rip out of the book and while I was being hauled away on a stretcher, I stuffed the scrap of paper into my mouth and swallowed. Someone had to rescue the proof of this connection and I knew that someone had to be me. It's my destiny. I see that clearly now. I'm the only one who has put it all together and I have to safeguard that knowledge until I can find a way to explore it further and then disseminate the information in a rational manner so that people believe me. No matter how ghastly a realization, humanity needs to know it's origins:

The Great Old Ones created the beehive-headed women—and all the other abominations the artwork in the book depicted—hundreds of thousands of years if not millions of years ago, to amuse themselves, because why else would they create anything so hideous, so inhumanly human? I remembered that the matriarchal books mentioned that these clay statues with obese female bodies and beehive heads were found in many places on the planet and dated to the same time frame, 25,000 B.C.E., pre-recorded history. But now I realized that those must have been the *only* clay figures to survive. What about the ones *before* those, that had to have disintegrated with time? That's when I made the final connection:

The Great Old Ones engineered these females long before 25,000 B.C.E., long before the cave paintings of 37,000 B.C.E. The females were around from the *beginning of time*. The Elder Gods had connected cells together, like the cells of a honeycomb, until they came up with this construction. Then the Great Old Ones impregnated them, as if they were rats in a lab experiment. Suddenly, in a flash of brilliance, I got it, how, they did this:

The Great Old Ones *also* created Neanderthals by combining and splicing cells and mated the beehive-headed women with the Neanderthals—more cells combining—just so they could see what would happen! The females gave birth over the millennia and those hybrids led to us! Evolving humanity. How much more apparent could it be?

These early women made little clay statues of each other, just like the cave painters replicated the animals they saw, just like the Great Old Ones painted or had painted the images of their horrifyingly distorted experiments, not human, not animal, not anything understandable! *These* are our ancestors! No wonder we're all insane!

All this grim knowledge lives in me now and the details are painfully clear, so obvious that it astonishes me that no one else has seen this! The beehive-headed women with the enormous bodies. Bodies that wouldn't have been obese if they were giants! Giants created as the first females who birthed what eventually became Homo sapiens, freakish mutants engineered somehow by gargantuan omnipotent aliens, the father-Gods of us all, that did nothing but entertain themselves, or maybe did things for a purpose we can't fathom but a purpose that wasn't loving. The incomprehensible archetypes that bequeathed us the legacy of soulless entertainment as a goal of life, like watching an endless string of cheap movies, wasting our precious time because our existence is pointless, meaningless and we are at the core, useless.

And then, they abandoned us, left us here on this planet to flounder, or *evolve*. It all makes so much sense and I know it's true. This knowledge is inside me now. I can see it's swelling my body as I have a hard time containing these facts. When I look in the mirror I see how much I resemble the obese beehive-headed figures whose voices buzz like a swarm of bees, creating sounds that form words in my head, each word nestled in its own little womb-like cell that is connected to the next little cell and the next to bind together and tell the story of the birth of homo Sapiens, a race that has no purpose, sired by gods that just didn't care. No wonder we're all crazy!

Always a Castle?

"We've always lived in the castle," Martin told me.

I glanced at him, a handsome if aloof man, late thirties maybe, who looked as if he rarely smiled. I turned back to face the enormous Tudor-Jacobean edifice that I would not have called a castle, more a small estate, although it did sport turrets.

Reddish brickwork had never appealed to me. This building material reminded me too much of PS 46 in the Bronx where I'd gone to grade school—but I did like the bay windows, and especially the little windows framing the front door. The wavy glass looked Tudor—I could tell by the green color—and I was amazed the panes had lasted over 500 years. "Since the castle was built, Dana," Martin assured me, as if reading my mind.

He insisted on a tour and I was pretty sure he'd be a good guide but I was zonked after such a long trip to Yorkshire. First there had been the six-hour flight from New York, an overnight near noisy Kings Cross tube station in London, then the early train to Leeds, where I was met at the station by a driver in one of those enormous old black Austin's that used to dominate the streets of London. The ride to Whaterley House took close to one hour and I curled up against the car's lush upholstery and stared out the window. Enchanting as I found the increasingly rural scenery to be, still, I managed a couple of cat naps.

At the entrance to the stately home I'd been greeted by Martin Whaterley, the nephew of Alexandra Whaterley, an aged widow in need of a companion who had selected me from "six hundred and sixty-six applicants" Martin's email quoted her as saying. I didn't know whether to believe that number and I vacillated between feeling flattered and frightened by such a picky employer.

This was not my dream job. My recently-acquired BA in history did not open doors to exciting work. To go for an MA with its promises of employment, well, I needed money. I definitely felt I had a grander purpose in life than taking care of a sick old woman in a remote location, but still, they'd paid for the trip to England, and the contract was short term and lucrative.

Martin took my coat down the hall and left my suitcases inside the door. The entrance area was large, with a grand staircase, overhead chandelier, black and white tiles beneath my feet, a Marketry Regency table under an oil painting of goats grazing in a field.

Martin was back quickly and I followed him on the enforced tour: the private parlor with what I judged to be a George II breakfront full of no-doubt pricey knick-knacks, and several damask-upholstered sofas with carved arms and legs; the library crammed floor to ceiling with leather-bound volumes which sheltered comfy-looking chairs; the 'drawing room' where presumably men used to smoke after dinner; the elegant dining room, set for a dozen dinner guests with ornate silver cutlery, crystal glassware and fine bone China rimmed in gold; the industrial kitchen—the only modern room I saw—all gleaming copper-bottomed pots hanging over the granite counter nestled in the middle of the latest stainless steel appliances; and finally the great hall that extended at the far end into a glassed-in atrium, this long and wide space crammed with walnut and ebony Queen Anne furniture, arranged to comprise seven living room groupings, and I wondered if this vast room was ever used. "We don't hold parties, because of auntie's advanced age. Just once a year, in the spring," Martin said, with that uncanny ability to guess my thoughts, or at least read my face, since clearly I was impressed by sideboards and silver tea services ready to accommodate a multitude of visitors.

Four large tapestries depicting Medieval-forest scenes hung from the walls. But most of the space was devoted to at least fifty gilded-framed portraits going back to what Martin assured me was "six generations, including the current generation, of course". These ancestors had been painted with downturned lips, beady eyes and severe expressions on their goat-like faces as they stood aggressively before pillars and thrones, or were presented in woodsy scenes with weapons and hunting dogs. I leaned in to the closest one to read the name on the brass plate: *Wilber Whaterley*. "My great great uncle, an American," Martin informed me.

I stared at Martin and blurted out, "You don't resemble your ancestors."

"Traits are often refined through natural selection," he said, with what I took to be a miniscule smile. Clearly the man knew his Darwin!

All of the portraits were of men and I wondered where the wives' images were stashed, but felt it a little too early to say anything controversial, other than, "Interesting features, your male ancestors," and left it to Martin to say more, but he didn't.

Instead, he led me up the massive oak staircase, the same polished wood used throughout the first floor, the steps lined with a faded Oriental runner, almost threadbare, and Martin nodded downward, saying, "This has been here only since the 1800s. The wood is original though, but furniture, drapes, carpeting have been added with each generation. Nothing has ever been removed, only added."

As we ascended, I noticed traces of a nasty odor, the smell getting sharper as we rose. We turned right and entered a door at the end of the hallway. My bags had been brought to this room by someone. The large space contained a Chinese Red lacquered dresser, a Louis XIV writing desk and accompanying walnut chair upholstered in red, an enormous gilded mirror above the desk, a black wrought-iron fireplace I could walk into if I felt like it, and a high narrow bed the length of which pressed against a wall. A gold filigreed *ciel de lit* attached above the bed, the red and rose gauzy curtain draped at the head and foot. A small wooden footstool had been placed beside the bed in order to climb up. Every wall was covered with flocked wallpaper—scarlet!— but for the wainscoting. The British would have said I was non-plussed; I would have called that an understatement. At least the smell wasn't so bad in here but I wanted to open a window.

"I understand you've a degree in antique decor," Martin said. That wasn't quite right—my major had been English history and antique furnishings had been a minor, not much more than a serious hobby. I decided on a smile instead of words because, again, I was feeling both overwhelmed and beat, and that smell was getting to me. Later, with the door shut and the old leaded casement open, I hoped I could air out the room.

"I've put you here, in what we call The Hell-Fire Chamber. A bit of family humor."

"Interesting," I said, not sure how to respond to that.

"Come, I'll show you Auntie Alexandra's rooms and you can meet her," Martin offered as, grim-faced, he led me back into the hallway, gesturing in a dismissive way as we passed a half dozen closed doors, saying, "There's nothing worth seeing in these."

I'd have *loved* to see what was inside. Among other favorites, I'm a huge fan of *petit point,* and mahogany Chippendale—I had spotted an ornate Chippy tilt-table in the great hall! I'd also seen a gorgeous embroidered three-person *indiscrète* settee there, obviously not dating back to the house's inception, but who cares!

As we walked down the long hallway towards the other end, I noticed the rank odor growing stronger. It was so foul that I found a tissue in my dress pocket and dabbed it at my nose, pretending I had the sniffles, an obvious and vapid attempt to disguise my revulsion. Martin didn't seem to notice my reaction, or even the smell for that matter, so I gave up discrete in favor of crude and just held the tissue to my nostrils. Still, as we walked along the hallway, the odor became overpowering and I felt an urge to gag but had the sense to control myself. *Nice reaction, Dana, your first day on the job!*

We reached the other end of the hallway, turned left, then went up six steps to a massive door. This area was so dark—no windows or lighting—that I couldn't make out the carvings in the wood. A horizontal crystal door handle was positioned in the dead center of the door; I'd only seen pictures of door handles—mostly knobs—in the centers of the enormous doors of eighteenth-century cathedrals. I leaned in and squinted. When I realized that the handle was shaped like an arm bone, I jerked back!

Martin knocked three times with one knuckle, so quietly I wondered if Mrs. Whaterley would hear him. He didn't wait for a response but pushed the bone handle down and the door creaked inward.

I found the source of the stink! It was so bad in there that I did gag, and clamped the tissue over my mouth too. Martin still didn't seem to notice as he led me further in.

We'd entered an almost lightless room. As my eyes adjusted, I figured this to be a kind of sitting room, the curtains drawn tight against the early afternoon sunlight and I couldn't make out anything but vague outlines of furnishings. We quickly passed through the open double doors into the large bedroom where the drapes were also closed. One fat pillar candle in a tall iron holder next to the double bed made a valiant attempt to pierce the darkness of this suite, but faced a losing battle. If it hadn't been for the stark white face, I probably wouldn't have noticed the small form lying on the bed, coverers pulled to above the chin. And despite knowing I was being rude, I held the tissue firmly over my nose and tried to breathe through my mouth with small breaths.

"Auntie, this is Ms. Dana Keenan, your new companion."

I expected a feeble response, or none at all, but a booming voice with a register low enough to be a baritone burst from the bed, "I know who in hell she is!"

I waited a respectful second but when Mrs. W did not acknowledge my presence, I suppressed my surging 'fuck you, lady!' attitude, removed the tissue from my nose, and said, "Hello, Mrs. Whaterley. It's a pleasure to meet you!"

"Is it?" the voice snapped. "We'll see what pleasure you feel in my presence."

This shocked me. Martin, who I could not see, said in a soft voice, "Auntie tires easily these days. We'd best keep this first meeting short."

To her he added in a louder and vaguely cheerful voice, as if the old lady was deaf and dumb—and I doubted she was either—"We'll go now, Auntie, so that Ms Keenan can get settled. Perhaps you can come down this evening and—"

"I'll come down if I feel like it and not if I don't!"

Martin reached out of the shadows and took my arm, turning me from the cranky old woman and leading me back through the sitting room. I'd brought the tissue up to my nose again, aware that the vile odor was now trapped in my sinuses. I desperately wanted to get outside for some fresh air.

Just as we reached the door, that voice reverberated through the two rooms and surrounded us. "I'll want attending to this night!"

My heart sank. I realized I could not do this job. I needed the work, and this was England after all—a real opportunity—and in such a bad economy I was lucky to even find a decent-paying job, but no matter how much I tried to dissuade myself, this was too much! The woman was nasty, and the rancid odor that clogged the air . . . No, I wouldn't be staying at Whaterley House!

I followed Martin to the first floor and as we reached the bottom of the stairs, I was about to tell him of my decision, and did manage to say, "Martin, I'd——"

That was as far as I got. He interrupted me with, "Come, Ms. Keenan—may I call you Dana?"

"Uh, yes, of course," I said, thinking, *You already have!*

"Let's walk through the grounds and I'll show you the gardens—we've prize-winning antique roses. It's crisp today. I'll get your coat."

Before I could respond, he vanished, leaving me standing at the entrance. I thought about how I could phrase my quick resignation without being either obnoxious or obtuse, because I had no intention of staying in this house even one night, let alone fulfilling a contract that spanned the better part of a year. That wasn't going to happen!

Martin returned with my coat and scarf and led me out the door to the flagstone walk where we turned right. This paved path wound away from the house and even from here I could see massive gardens ahead. All the while Martin chatted about the construction of the garden by Capability Brown in the 1700s, the maze at its epicenter, expanded over the centuries, the variety of flowers and shrubs. I've never

been able to identify flowers, unless they appeared on upholstery, but I knew what I found visually beautiful and pleas-
antly scented, and this garden was both.

We stopped at the Heirloom roses, only one miraculously
still in bloom. "The weather turned a fortnight ago," Martin
said, again exhibiting his uncanny skill of mind-reading.
"Flowers, unfortunately, die from the cold. But the bushes
are perennials, you know. Each spring they bring forth new
life."

He bent and snapped the stem of the single white rose
still in bloom, and for some reason that aggressive act
seemed violent to me, destroying the last living thing in this
bed of decay.

He turned and handed it to me, his ashen eyes still expressionless, his lips an even straight line, as if they were
incapable of turning either up or down. I found his benign
face mesmerizing and absently reached out to take the rose.

And cried out as pain shot through my fingertip! I jerked
my hand away from the thorn and blood flecks splattered
the flower's pristine petals.

"Be careful!" Martin snapped, his voice a sudden imita-
tion of Mrs. Whaterley's in tone, depth and annoyance, and
I glanced at his face. "We don't want you infected!" His eyes
had turned steely, his look so intense I had to turn away.

I glanced toward the house and saw movement at the
corner of an upstairs window and suspected it was Mrs.
Whaterley, watching.

All of this so unnerved me that I blurted out, "Martin,
I'm really sorry, but I can't take the job. I'm not the right
person to be your aunt's companion."

His eyes settled into the flat grey and he said in an even
voice, "But, Dana, you've come all this way. Surely you
might give the position a chance."

He sounded so reasonable and I realized I'd had a tinge

of hysteria in my voice. I tried to calm my tone. "You have hundreds of resumés. You'll find someone else, I'm sure." Why was I trying to reassure *him*!

As if on cue, thunder rumbled overhead and the sky darkened quickly. "I think we'd best retreat to the house," he said, firmly grasping my upper arm and leading me back quickly.

We had to run the last hundred yards when a cloud burst soaked us.

"Here," he said when the door closed, "let's get that wet coat off." As he did this, I felt his body behind mine, too close, his cool breath on my damp neck, and I shivered with an unknown fear.

Suddenly he moved a step back. "I'll bring a towel."

When I turned, he handed me the rose, saying, "Between the thorns should prove less painful."

Like a child, I took the rose and stood inside the entrance hair dripping, shoes squishing water, staring at the white petals tainted with small dots of my very red blood. Suddenly a deeper chill swept over me. This house was dangerous! I don't know how I knew this, and I refused to analyze the thought: *I want out!*

Instead of waiting for Martin to return, I placed the rose on the hallway table and, shivering, ran up the stairs to my room. My bags were still packed and I picked them up, moving out the door and into the hall towards the stairs.

And stopped dead at the sight before me. Out of the gloom from the opposite end of the corridor a diminutive form, pale as a ghost, swaddled in white like a mummy, floated quickly towards me. Bringing with it the noxious odor!

I took two steps back and instinctively my eyes squeezed tightly closed to block out this rank apparition.

You're imagining this! I told myself. I opened my eyes

slowly to find inches from my chin a long, goat-like face with hairs sticking out here and there, the features twisted in fury, the skin puckered and pale as a corpse, the glassy black eyes staring malevolently at me. The odor was beyond impossible and I gagged and jerked back, banging the heaviest suitcase into my shin.

The downturned lips parted and it was as if an impossibly black, fetid cavity opened, one that would go on forever. The odor was the same as I'd smelled in her room, something from the other side of death, and the word *Evil!* popped into my head. Horrified and frozen to the spot, because she was so close, I was forced to breathe in that odor, and sensed I was inhaling poison!

I stared, nearly mesmerized as her lips formed the words: "I will come below tonight and you will join me. Below." Her voice was as deep as before and suddenly I wasn't sure if this was a woman or a man.

Stunned, I could only nod, half paralyzed by terror.

"Prepare yourself!" she snapped, the tone beyond harsh and demanding.

Too frightened to speak, I backed up several steps, then turned and ran into my room, slamming then locking the door behind me. I leaned against the door gasping for air, shaking with fear, confused, doubting what had just happened.

This is ridiculous! I told myself. *What did you see? An old woman with the voice of a man, eccentric, smelly, that's all. She acts like a queen, this matriarch, clearly used to being obeyed.*

But I had no intention of obeying! I decided to wait for a few minutes, crack the door to make sure the coast was clear, then get away from this house. Even if I had to *walk* back to the station in the downpour, I was leaving Whaterley House with its repulsive smells and creepy people. Let them hire applicant 665!

Suddenly, a rush of heat filled my body from my toes to my head and sweat gushed from every pore. My head felt light and empty and I had to sit down. I dropped the one suitcase I was still holding and staggered to the bed, stepping on the little stool to sit. The dizziness increased and with it I went from hot to cold as a chill stabbed my body. I shivered, at first mildly, then uncontrollably, and crawled under the covers, wishing I had more blankets, wishing there was a fire in the fireplace, shaking so much my teeth chattered.

I'm sick, I thought. *How can I be sick?* And then I lost awareness, slipping in and out of sleep, of dreams and hallucinations. Between freezing and burning, I drifted through time. Someone must have entered the room and built a fire in the fireplace: yellow-orange-red flames licked the black screen as if trying to reach me, wood crackled, too loud, a tree felled by lightening. Heat raged, scorching the room, making the air wavy to my vision, barely touching my icy, trembling flesh. Then, suddenly, I was engulfed, kicking off the blankets, my body on the verge of igniting.

The flocked wallpaper's raised velvet became blood-red figures, alive, squiggling like maggots, swarming all around me! I felt so depleted I couldn't move to escape. All I seemed capable of doing was emitting low, wretched sounds, cries of dread. My world had turned into a nightmare. But the worst was yet to come.

At my weakest, most vulnerable point, Mrs. Whaterley appeared. This . . . creature stared down at me, crinkly animal-face severe, black-hole eyes glinting, downturned lips shifting into something like a wicked smile that parted into a black expanding abyss. I trembled and sobbed, wishing I could sleep to ward off the sight of this abomination. I did close my eyes. That was a mistake. When I opened them, she was still there, but the shroud no longer encased her. The naked body was a shock, forcing a gasp then a scream from me, one that reverberated inside my head. What loomed above and reached out for me, not an old woman, or even an old man. This was no human being! The bony torso protruding against death-white flesh, skin wrinkled and layered like centuries of erosion, this . . . thing . . . I can only call it a *thing* . . . had a dozen arms! But they *weren't* arms, they were appendages without hands, extending from its back, weaving and swaying like the maggots in the wallpaper. And now all of those arms came at me!

The shock of this abhorrent touch left me screaming, vomiting, choking, gasping for air, suffocating, incoherent. Suddenly Martin was there, behind her, then in front of her, then she was gone. He lifted me up, pounding my back so I could breathe, holding me upright, telling me to relax, and I realized I was naked. "Where . . . is it?" I stuttered. "The arms . . ."

"There, there," Martin said, in an attempt to be comforting in his distant way. "Drink this," he said, and turned to reach for a cup of tea. In that moment I glanced down at my naked body and saw blood between my legs. And screamed, "Help me! Help me escape!"

"You're not a prisoner, Dana. You can leave, if you're strong enough. Right now, you're weak. You'll need to rebuild your strength for the coming months."

"What do you mean? What are you talking about?" I shrieked. I sounded incoherent and I had no idea if he understood me because he didn't answer. I only knew that as much as I longed to leave Whaterley House, I could not move.

My fever lasted days, weeks, I don't know, I lost track of time. When it was most intense, the thing called Mrs. Whaterley visited me. While I struggled to stay conscious, all I could remember was the handless tentacle-arms reaching for me, touching my bare skin with an otherworldly iciness. And the blood, afterwards. Always the blood.

When the fever finally broke and I came back to myself, I wrapped up in the comforter stinking of sweat and other things and managed to get out of bed, dizzy as I stood, my head empty, but I was determined. I needed to get out of here!

I staggered to the window and saw fields covered with snow! How much time had passed? My legs were weak and I had to sit. On the small table beside the chair sat a plate of fruit, some bread and butter, a tea pot, cup and saucer. Also on the table was the white rose flecked with my blood, now withered, dried, in a vase with no water, the thorns in death still sharp.

A soft knock at my door made me cringe and pull the cover tighter around me. Without my answering, Martin came in.

"I'm delighted to see you're feeling better," he said, his tone even, his face showing no signs of delight. "I'll help you dress and you can come down for sustenance."

"I don't want to go downstairs and I don't want dinner," I said. "I want to leave."

Martin ignored me. He went to the armoire and selected one of my flower-print dresses—apparently someone had unpacked my bags.

He walked to me and said, "Stand, please."

"No! Leave me alone."

"You're very weak, Dana. Please don't struggle. You need to come down."

But I did struggle, pointlessly. Despite his slim frame, he was incredibly strong and quickly had me unwrapped from the comforter and the dress over my naked body.

Rebelliously, I whined, "I need underwear!"

"You don't," he said, like a parent to a child.

He pushed my feet into the shoes I'd worn on my arrival and then lifted me from the chair, half carrying me out the door, along the hallway and down the steps of the main staircase. Instantly, I was keenly aware of the foul smell— it was gone!

As if reading my thoughts, Martin said, "My aunt has had a turn for the better. Things have normalized."

"Normalized?!" I muttered as we reached the ground floor.

Instead of turning towards the dining room, we entered the great hall with the paintings of the severe ancestors. The room was so vast that at first, I didn't notice Mrs. Whaterley, or who or whatever she was, seated in the middle of the red-velvet three-person *indiscrète* settee.

Now, she looked almost normal to my eyes, an old lady, her thin, pointed face resembling that of her progenitors. She was wrapped in a large velvet cloak of a robe, her diminutive figure nearly swallowed by the settee on which she sat.

"Sit there," Martin said, and, exhausted, I dropped onto the seat on her right. Martin took the one to her left. The snake-like settee meant we could all look at one another easily, and around the room. Despite the pretense of dinner, we sat silently, me dozing now and then through the dark hours until dawn, at which point Martin stood and helped his aunt up and they left the room.

This is your chance! I told myself. *You might only get one!* I moved as quickly as my depleted frame could to the front door, flung it open, and stared at the snow blowing wildly across the walks and garden. The wind sweeping through the skeletons of shrubs, trees and hedges howled. How could I escape? The station was an hour away by car, half a day by foot. I was trapped here!

From behind me came the cold, even voice I'd grown to

loathe. "Only trapped for nine months," Martin said.

What was he talking about? A sudden awareness descended and I realized that inside me life was growing. How had that happened? Martin must have raped me when I was unconscious with fever. I hated him in that moment and spun to face him.

His face seemed to shift, taking on the features of his ancestors, and in an instant I knew what had *really* happened to me. To preserve my sanity, I blocked it out in a split second, the reality too horrifying to fully comprehend. All I let myself know was this: I was pregnant. I was not ready to face the rest of the horror.

Martin said I would be trapped for nine months, but he also said nothing ever leaves here, nothing is taken away, the roses die but the bush brings forth new life in the spring. Nine months from now it would be spring. At that moment, I realized that the moment I had set foot in Whaterley House, my fate was sealed.

Knowing that Martin could read me too well, I turned away and blocked thoughts of revenge. But this . . . creature . . . within me, if I could help it, it would never be born. I would not add to this dynasty of grotesques!

My days are spent alone in the Hell-Fire Room. I sleep, write this journal which I hide under the mattress, sleep more, stare out the window at the endless winter. Martin brings meals to me before sunset and after sunrise. Each night I am forced to join the Whaterley's on the *indiscrète*.

I bide my time, planning two things: My escape; The murder of these alien creatures. I must escape soon—the longer I wait, the harder it will be; my body is growing large and heavy, and the storms outside rage. I *must* escape because I know once the thing draws breath, they will bury me in the rose garden with the other dead roses who came before me, the human women used to evolve the line of this hideous 'family' of non-humans so that they *appear* human. But they are not. These are cold, alien beings, without sympathy, without empathy, without human kindness. Their cold kills.

There are monsters in our world, and I have come to understand my higher calling. I have amassed a small arsenal of tools, spending my hours alone sharpening pieces of wood, honing dinner knives, collecting shards of pottery I shatter until the edges are as sharp as scalpels.

I may or may not succeed in killing all three of them. I may or may not escape. If you're reading this, know that I will try.

One thing I have learned and what humanity needs to understand: there is an ancient, savage line, one not from Earth. I've figured out that they've existed all over the world, throughout time, even before the first homo Sapiens evolved. These . . . *things* . . . are bent on propagating, populating the planet with their kind in the guise of our kind. I don't know their final goal, but what I'm absolutely certain of is this: their end will lead to our end!

Cold Comfort

James felt caught by the frozen tension of a Montreal winter. He lingered in the hotel dining room over a late meal, but still did not feel sleepy. After dessert, he decided on a walk before heading to bed.

As James left the hotel, icy air wounded him. He adjusted the collar of his grey wool coat. Head bowed, he moved west into the wind, toward Crescent Street.

Snow drifts lining the gutter had frozen into dirty mounds that would be difficult to scale. He hoped the full force of the storm would hold off until after his departure.

Few cars moved along the street empty of pedestrians. While walking, James focused on an enormous machine noisily eating its way through the impacted ice. As the slow-moving monster consumed solids, it excreted only a dribble of liquid from its opposite end. Transformation took place deep within that gargantuan belly, hidden, and it surprised James, who prided himself on rarely indulging in idle speculation, that he was questioning the process.

His thoughts shifted to demographics and target markets. Glancing at his watch, he pictured Millie and the boys skating at the community rink. He hoped she had remembered to take the car in for winterizing.

Sharp wind demanded awareness of his surroundings. He heard what sounded like a hinge squeaking and turned his head. Amid the glow of imaginative displays in brightly-lit shop windows, a darkened doorway stood out. He suspected this was where the noise originated. When Arctic air slashed his cheek, interest in the doorway faded. *Tomorrow's a busy day*, he thought. *I'd better head back.*

Again the squeak galvanized his impulse to look. He heard other sounds emitted from the blackness, reminiscent of a primitive language. He thought he could make out the words, *"Le change?"*

"Le change?" he echoed, insecure about his French. He glanced behind, afraid to be discovered talking to himself.

"Change," a voice said in English. "You know."

A tremor of stupidity passed through James. Gusts of snow eroded that feeling, buffeting him until he could barely keep balanced. When the current shifted, he faced the doorway, eyes narrowed. "You mean you want money."

The wind stilled and another sound reached his ears: bark crackling in fire, a scalp being scratched, raspy laughter. Through swirling snow, he watched a hand emerge from the darkness, palm up. Each finger of the split glove revealed soiled flesh. The hand withdrew so quickly it was as though it had never existed.

James knew that at home he would not be exposed in this way. Street people, he had convinced himself, are a city phenomenon, relegated to the downtown core where life congeals. On the rare occasions when he encountered them--business trips and vacations--he usually crossed the street, avoiding contact.

He felt as much responsibility as anyone. But there were places for the unfortunate, organizations to help. He contributed to charities. Once his wife drove half an hour into a seedier part of the city taking a bag of canned goods to a food bank after hearing a plea on the radio. *I'm not cold-hearted*, he reassured himself, *but you have to draw the line somewhere.*

"I suppose you want it for coffee, or a sandwich," he said, feeling uncomfortable.

A rumble attracted him. Another machine turned the corner. Bulky, oddly tentacled, tires large and deep-threaded. Methodically it sprayed salt crystals along the ice-slicked asphalt. He watched as the awkward vehicle lumbered, struggling to reestablish traction.

"Coffee? Don't touch the stuff."

James shivered and stamped his feet. His gut constricted. Trapped between instincts, he endured paralysis for several moments until he heard, "Not food neither."

Paralysis gave way to savagery. "You want it for alcohol!"

Quickly James glanced left then right. The street was still empty.

"Nope, not booze."

A long-forgotten feeling surfaced: fury at being toyed with. Madness brushed him. *There's still work to do*, he reminded himself. *Tomorrow's going to be hectic.* Sleep beckoned.

He began walking east but before snow had crunched under both of his feet he heard, "It's this book I gotta read."

Incredulous, James turned. He stared at the blackened building entrance but still could discern nothing.

A bus drove close to the curb. Distracted, he peered into eight passing windows, eight rectangular eyes inviting him to view a contained world. Two pale, heavily-bundled figures, resigned to the elements, sat at opposite ends of the vehicle. When the bus was gone and silence restored, James glanced down. He was annoyed to find the bottom of his coat stained.

"Costs twelve ninety-five new," came the scratchy words, "but it's an old story."

"You're a derelict! Why am I talking to you?" his voice boomed in his ears. As James restrained himself, again the cold seeped in.

"Andrea 'round the block's got it used for five fifty."

The unwanted explanation had an odd effect and a glacial force threatened to engulf James. A small groan slipped from between his chilled lips.

"I'm done *L'Étranger*. You know it?"

"What? . . ." *The Stranger?* by Camus? James was afraid to hear more.

Quickly he pulled off one glove and reached into his coat pocket. "I won't give you all of it." He had intended to present the words as controlled, justifiably gruff, but they hung in the air like cheap and silly plastic icicles.

Still, James could not stop himself. "Why should I subsidize your reading?" he grumbled. "Go to the library if you want a book."

He opened his wallet and sorted through the bills, finding a five and a ten, plucking out the former. With his vulnerable hand he extended the money, aware his skin was freezing.

The hand reached out again from darkness into illumination. It was followed by an arm, only to the elbow, and James fell back. Rotted coat sleeve. Matted fabric adhering to wrist and palm. Ancient gnarled fingers, three bare to the knuckles, quivering. Gritty, jagged nails.

The fingers snatched the money. Although that flesh had barely touched his own, James was grateful for the temporary loss of feeling. He watched the arm, the hand and finally the bill vanish into the shadows.

Quickly he shoved his own numbed hand back into the leather glove, then under his armpit, hugging himself. Alarmed by reviving sensation, he longed for comfort. Maybe he would hail a taxi back to the hotel. The street was deserted.

He felt foolish. Gullible. Allowing himself to become upset. *What possessed me?* he wondered, shaking his head.

Quickly James turned from the doorway muttering,

"That will have to do!" and hurried away, unaccountably relieved that no gratitude had been shown.

Even before daybreak, the storm ended. Montreal's snowy streets glistened in the blinding winter sun. Cars and pedestrians crowded the downtown, reinjecting vitality into the city.

With a good night's sleep to carry him through, James was off early to meetings that lasted the morning and much of the busy afternoon.

Twice during the day he astonished himself by idly speculating about the book. Of course, he had read *The Outsider* when he was at university, but he could not recall what it was about.

He checked out of the hotel and ate a hurried late lunch at a coffee bar, wanting to catch the five o'clock flight. He could be home by eight.

That night, safe in his own bed, Millie snuggled close, the boys asleep down the hall, James jolted awake. Hot sweat burned his flesh. His heart rammed his chest wall. Layers of sweltering shadow wrapped his world in unfamiliarity. He did not recognize this woman lying beside him. He did not recognize himself.

He made his way downstairs to the den. Seated at his desk, the gun lockbox open, the weapon in his hand pointing away from him, toward him, away, toward . . .

Stasis. What could be yet never would be! Such crystal clarity left him aching for that cold, numbing comfort.

Death Dreaming

I dreamed you were dead. That's not so unusual. People dream others are dead all the time, people they love, people they hate, people they don't even know or care about. And they dream that they themselves are dead, mostly when they freefall—that's a classic. Death is the end of life so it's human nature to think about this, both waking and sleeping. And to worry. That's all normal; at least Dr. Howard believes it is.

I dream often that you're dead—well, *dying*, right at the brink of death, ready to tip. Once a week I dream this; if I'm being really truthful, sometimes more than that.

The first time I dreamt you were dying was just after Julie passed. Dr. Howard said her death triggered it, and assured me that's not uncommon. I can still see you hanging by your fingertips from the marquee over the entrance to the Trump Tower Hotel in NYC where we stayed the week of the funeral. You had your head turned and tilted, gazing down at the sidewalk, at me. It wasn't a long drop to the ground—maybe twenty-five feet—and I wondered if such a fall would end in death or just a few broken bones. Maybe lifelong paralysis? For those reasons, I didn't take the remarkably ridiculous situation seriously at all, that first dream. As always in these dreams, as I would come to experience them, I stared at you as you pleaded with your eyes, begging me for help. For me, it was/is a dilemma. I never know if you're asking me to rescue you from the jaws of death, or to shove you into the Grim Reaper's maw and get it over with. You've always had a sense of humor, and I laughed.

That first dream, I turned and walked away. And then jolted awake, as if something in my head had exploded. I sat up in the darkness, trembling, heart pounding, head throbbing, the dreamworld still vivid and immediate, my guilt palpable—I'd let you down. Again.

Since then, whenever I've dreamed of your death, I have not turned away early. I've stayed to watch until the end, as if it's a movie and I just have to see how it will conclude. But I always wake just before the finale.

I've realized that it's better to watch, wait, see if one of us will come to a decision. I wait. You wait. That long pause is always fraught with tension and I know if either of us moves, something will happen. One of us will snap. Maybe both of us.

Over the last year I've dreamt so many different scenarios of your demise and in truth, despite the horror, it's kind of fun and invigorating every night as I go to sleep anticipating, wondering if I'll dream about your death again, wondering what it will be like *this* time. The big picture is always the same, but the details are unique.

Once, you held a gun to your temple. It was a big handgun, the kind cowboys regularly aimed at one another in the westerns we watched on TV as kids. A Colt .45, if I remember my *Trivial Pursuit* answers correctly from when we used to play the game with Julie. A romantic gun, because of actors like John Wayne. In the dream, the TV was on in the background and the old movie *Rio Grande* played, the sound muted. The radio in the next room blared out current insta-news, something about the Middle East. Your features were etched with grief and fear, maybe for the refugees of the most recent conflict, but probably not. You probably didn't care about the refugees, or about cowboys or even care about the grief I saw reflected in your eyes. Your hand shook but your finger was steady and clearly poised over the trigger. All the while you stared at me, that pleading look. Should I stop you or should I wait to catch the final shootout? I waited to see what would happen. And then I woke up.

Another time it was a knife, a large one, the kind they use in abattoirs, the religious ones that still manually slit the throats of food animals. A knife also good for boning, I imagine, very sharp. In that dream you wore a chef's apron and the white hat and I thought you looked absurd with copper-bottomed pots and pans hanging over your head and the array of culinary tools pegged to a board behind you. Absurd because you *never* liked to cook. Which was why it came as no surprise that you dropped out of the one cooking class you enrolled in.

You held the blade of the big knife to your throat, as if you were a bovine about to be slaughtered then rendered and eventually appearing on a dinner table. Your eyes seemed large in that dream, liquid-filled, conscious cow eyes, so unlike your hazel orbs, but still familiar. Eyes imploring. For what? I waited, but then I woke up without ever knowing what you wanted, what I could do, what you would do.

There are many more mundane dreams, all familiar means of dispatch: strangulation, hanging, drowning, gassing, even disease in the final stages. Nothing spectacular or unusual. Some of the weapons were a bit more interesting than others, even amusing: The $200 goose down 500-thread Egyptian cotton pillow you bought on a whim two years ago and which Julie joked might suffocate you while you slept— positioned over your nose and mouth in the dream; the taser you pressed against your cheek as lightning zapped through the air Tesla-style, waiting for a bolt to hit the gun and amp up the voltage; the axe that you used to chop wood against a tree stump during that god-awful ice-storm winter when you lived in a century-old farm house you rented, ostensibly to paint, yet produced only one painting—of the severed chipmunk you claimed you 'accidentally' axe-murdered. Oh, and there were those silly nun chucks and throwing stars you played with in your last year of high school, the matching set in black, red and silver, etched and highly ornate, the stars extremely sharp. You never did get the hang of these Oriental weapons and many times bashed your skull with one of the wooden handles, or sliced into your fingertips with the razor-stars.

All of these and many other weapons made it into my dreams of your death. Bits and pieces of a life, scattered like ripped-up photographs littering the ground, fragments of memories with no rhyme or reason, no connections made except to someone who knows you well, and that someone is, unfortunately, me.

For that reason alone, I think my favorite dream involved poison. Nothing icky like an insect or snake or arachnid bite—although there *was* the Black Widow dream, but I digress. No, this poison was one of the no-mess powders or liquids that dissolve in food or drink and leave little or no trace. Poisons have always been a joint interest of ours, and we've explored the idea of ingesting a substance so lethal that life comes to an end before the toxin makes it to the stomach. Quick. Or slow. Agony or ecstasy. In that dream, next to you on the round mahogany table sat Julie's Brown Betty teapot you inherited, and a China cup and saucer— the set with the silver around the rim—, a wedge of lemon on the saucer, the way you prefer tea. "Oh So Agatha Christie!" Julie used to laugh! Also on the small table was a tiny, opaque bottle, as brown as the teapot, it's yellowing label hand-scripted with the word 'Poison' carefully lettered above the stereotypical skull-and-crossed bones. The bottle struck me as from the late 1800s and looked very much like the one we found in Portobello Market on a trip to London. Its contents might have been laudanum, but that couldn't be right because you wouldn't die from a teaspoon's worth of laudanum in your tea, which is all that small bottle would have held. Besides, laudanum is only one percent morphine, after all, and you didn't look drugged, at least not drugged in the euphoric sense. I suspect that little bottle crying out 'Poison' contained something more lethal. Arsenic? Too 'old lace,' and not quick enough. Potassium cyanide? I did not smell bitter almond—the dreams have always been multi-sensory. Besides, you would already be dead. An overdose of Digitalis, then? But, where is the Foxglove? And clearly you are not suffering a heart attack. Perhaps Ricin from the flowering *Ricinus communis* depicted in the painting on the wall behind you that you created one year ago in Julie's garden. The seeds within the gorgeous red, spiky-fuzzy balls of the Castor Oil plant produce Ricin and in this death scene your teacup is empty but for leaves, the tea already drunk, and now you will be gone in no time, or, the usual amount of time. In this dream, I tried hard to decipher what you're asking for, and if I'm willing to give it, but I could not.

I don't mind the variations on the types of death; at least I'm not bored in my sleep. It's really that baffling look in your eyes, always the same, always open to interpretation. Are you begging to be left alone to die in misery or in peace, or are you asking for the antidote, or rejecting it? You've always been like this, caught between things, between life and death, and consequently waiting for someone else to either rescue you, or harm you. But then, so have I. Decisions are difficult and exhausting. Choices confusing. We were not taught how or encouraged to make decisions and passivity reigned in our upbringing. You know that truth as well as I do.

So, what does my therapist say about all this? *Dr. Howie,*

as he prefers to be called, takes a Freudian interpretation one week, a Jungian slant the next, and throws in a bit of biofeedback to go with the anti-depressants he prescribes. Here's what he has said:

—You are worried about your own, impending demise. (*obvious*)

—You are searching for spiritual answers, a way to make sense of life and death. (*sure*)

—You have unresolved issues around Julie's death. (*no kidding!*)

—You seem (*insert emotion: angry; sad; jealous; happy; in mourning*)

The dreams have become more frequent. Last night's drama was the third this week, and it was a doozie. You were in the far north, the Yukon perhaps, a place we always wanted to visit, the temperature sub-zero, both Celsius and Fahrenheit. The scene was a bit Jack London, a white waste-land, bitter, cutting wind, ice crystals layered on eyebrows and eyelashes, your down-filled coat warm but not warm enough. I expected to see sled dogs murdered for their fur, hands thrust into their entrails for warmth. Or wolves circling, sniffing out prey. But it was only you, propped against the lone, barren tree, slowly becoming buried beneath the relentlessly falling snow as the wind howled like a banshee. And yet I could only think: the air is so crisp and glacially clean!

You wore fleece mitts and in one of them clutched the largest icicle I'd ever seen, the length and thickness of a long, fat dagger or short sword. Death by icicle! I laughed and then saw that look in your eyes and knew I had to take this seriously. You were so bundled up, though, I couldn't imagine how you could dispatch yourself until, suddenly, I realized you wore no goggles. It was a horrifying thought, but I also wondered if the icicle would melt before a decision had to be made, one way or the other. Probably not in this extreme temperature. No, the cold was like the frigidity of our lives, we, the perpetually-frozen Charlottes, in stasis, unable to move. And so I waited. You waited. And then I awoke.

Today, Dr. Howie said:

—A perfect murder weapon, ice. (*the world ends in fire or . . .*)

—Rather far-fetched. (*you think?*)

—The metaphor, the symbolism, that's what's important. (*the symbolic cold reflects the real-life cold. did I get that right, doc?*)

This afternoon I had a sudden recall of that childhood summer we spent by the seashore in Wildwood. It was a peculiar apartment the adults rented, three bedrooms in a row, railroad boarding house style, a kitchen and bathroom at the back.

The colors made the apartment a curiosity. The first room was completely pink, pink as a sunburn, everything, the carpet, the walls, the bedspread and lampshades and chair seats . . . The second blue as the cool Atlantic Ocean, the same, everything in the room blue . . . The third bedroom was yellow, blindingly so, resembling the landscape as the glaring sun beat down on us . . .

Our summer abode was situated on the narrow street across from the beach and we were drawn to the water daily, with Julie, from morning until the sun began to set. The adults were happy to be left alone, a routine check periodically, a command to use sunscreen, to not go too far into the ocean because there might be an undertow that would drag us out to sea. I always wondered what it would be like to be dragged out to sea. Would it be painful to die engulfed and then drawn down into the murky depths with the jellyfish and flounders, caught by seaweed, losing limbs to sharks, a victim of the powerful salt water? What would be the last experience?

That day, I stepped out of my childhood comfort zone and verbalized my thoughts, only to be met with silence. And what was there to say? Then? Now?

In my mind I can still hear the waves crashing as they broke. I loved watching the white crests form, from the right, from the left, meeting in the middle, the momentum forcing the fracture, salty water rushing to our ankles, up our legs, sucking us into the sand as it retreated.

The sand back then was clean all the time, a beige non-color, crystalline and bright beneath the brilliant sun that cooked Julie's skin pink and then red. Her pale, fragile flesh did not tan, just burned, then blistered painfully, the nights permeated by the scent of Noxzema, and her sobs. But, she would not leave the sunshine. She refused to leave us.

We of hardier stock, skin like a rhino, prone to darkening, the sun our friend to the extent it was Julie's enemy. We did not even think about sending her to safety.

—"Curious," Doctor Howie ventured when I conveyed this memory. (*perhaps*)

—"I believe Julie died of melanoma. Damage from childhood exposure?" (i *get it!*)

—"How do you feel about that?" (*helpless, of course. always helpless*)

—"I think we are getting somewhere with the connections." (*do you? is it such a mystery?*)

I left his office in defeat and called after hours when I knew he would be gone to leave a message cancelling my follow-up appointment. For once I crawled into bed battling neither dread nor anticipation. My mind felt unclouded, my heart unburdened. What would be would be, and, as always, events were beyond my feeble control.

I close my eyes to sleep. I dream. But you are not in the dream, just a plethora of the various scenes, weapons a slide-show. Heat and chill on my flesh, scent of sweet fragrances and foul odors, sounds of waves and blaring horns and desperate, painful cries. I am trapped in a revolving sensory mosaic with snatches from all the dreams of your death, and suddenly I am afraid.

Frantically, I search for you, fearful I will not find you, my stress escalating, the pressure in my chest and my head expanding at a dangerous rate . . .

And then, there you are!

The past-dream fragments give way to a locale that is not exotic, and it is not a place I recognize from where we have been or have wanted to go. It is visually sharp, like the setting in a movie, a picture from a travel brochure. You stand in a field of Kelly-green grass on a mid-summer's day, the cap of azure above strewn with pristine clouds, gilded sunlight glinting off your hair and forming a body aura, your hazel eyes intense, as always.

There are no weapons visible. Nothing and no one stands beyond you or between us. You stare at me, the familiar intimacy in your eyes pulling me towards you, pushing me away; the unspoken plea.

And in a split second it comes to me, psychically knocking me over as would physically a powerful wave, a ferocious wind, the blast of a handgun fired point-blank. Finally, *finally*, I get it!

We have grown so close, you and I, co-joined. Close enough to become as one. I believed that one night I would understand what you wanted. What you needed. What you have always needed. And now I do.

In this moment of luminosity you realize that I am certain now, and the look in your eyes alters. You can see with clarity what I've been seeing all along.

We wait. We watch. We tremble.

You are morphing into the vivid colors, the pungent scents, the reverberating sounds from dreams. To my utter joy and stark horror, impacted by eternal grief, before me is what I have always feared: evolution in a world of death-dreaming leads to evanescence. I watch you disappear . . .

Eye of the Beholder

She will never be the same. She knows that, accepts it. Life once made sense, but not now. Why did she listen to them? But it was *her* actions, right from the start, *her* making wrong decisions . . . It was as if she had intentionally entered a rank, twisting tunnel that drew vermin, narrowing, becoming ever more grave-like the farther in she went, burying her alive with the awareness of . . . of this . . . this . . . abomination . . .

At the beginning, it hadn't been the intervention that bothered Liz, it was the fervor, the wild, ecstatic gleam in the eyes of her sister, her cousin, her best friend. She'd wondered why they were so avid about changing her but let it pass as caring.

"It's not life or death, you know!" she reminded them several times, progressively hearing her voice weaken as they brought up counter arguments.

Her best friend Marti was the voice of reason that rang in her ears afterwards: "Liz, it *is* life or death! Do you want to die single? Childless?"

"I'm thirty-eight. Not exactly over the hill."

"Your best days are *right this minute*," her cousin Phyllis said. "It doesn't get any better from here. I should know."

Liz wanted to say, *Phyllis, you're only forty-eight, just ten years older than me. You're not exactly ready for an old-age home!* But whatever protests she had mounted over the last two hours had been countered with the same basic argument—if she didn't get married soon and start having kids,

'Which,' they all were only too happy to reminder her 'you say you want,' it will be 'over.' And they had a point. She did want those things. Badly. And time *was* slipping by.

She'd brought up, "Well, Mom had me when she was forty-three, and I'm okay." The silence had been deafening. That they all thought she *wasn't* 'okay' unnerved her.

"This is silly," Liz said, reaching for a breadstick on the coffee table laden with healthy food. She plunged one end into the sour cream and onion dip. Instantly, Phyllis grabbed the breadstick from her hand and hissed at her.

Liz sighed. "Okay, okay, I give up! I'll go for a stupid facial."

"You'll go for derma abrasion!" Marti said.

"And Botox!" Phyllis ordered.

"You want me to have botulism injected into my——"

"And fills. Don't forget the collagen fills," Marti added. "That will get those wrinkles and sags out of your pouchy cheeks and give you the plumpness of youth."

"I thought you said I'm too fat," Liz snapped.

"Not fat, sweetie, just, well, you could stand to lose ten pounds and be better off for it."

Liz looked longingly at the breadsticks and heard her stomach rumble in sympathy. She hadn't eaten since lunch and now it was after 8 P.M. Maybe if she just agreed to everything, they'd let her have a grape!

"Look, Lizzie, hon, we're all on your side, you know." This from her perfect twin sister Tiffany. Slim, well quaffed, stylishly dressed, glamorous or sophisticated—depending on the day—birthing a son named Jim, Jr. at thirty-one and more recently the mother of triplet girls. "Men have gotten *very* picky over the last couple of decades, and scarce. Every male and female on the planet knows exactly what they want."

Liz wondered what deep knowledge Tiffany could possess with the same not-yet-four-decades under her belt, one of them childhood. She hadn't even dated until college! They might be twins, but they were so different, the two of them, so how could she take advice from her *kid* sister by three minutes who seemed to have everything and—

"Look what I had to do to get my Jim! What I do to keep him."

"True," Phyllis said. "You're not a slippers and robe kinda girl."

Tiffany shrugged. "I like to look good. So sue me. But it gets me what I want."

Liz wondered what was so wondrous about Jim, a tall, *GQ* handsome guy with a fake smile full of thirty-two perfect teeth and a seven-figure income that kept him out of the house seven days most weeks, presumably in his office at the brokerage firm, but who could be sure. And apparently Tiffany didn't care.

But Liz realized that she was jealous of her sister. Besides having the life she wanted, Tiffany had only worked for five years—as a fast-living flight attendant, which is where she met Jim. Liz, on the other hand, had been relegated to curatorial assistant in the entomology department of the natural history museum's basement for the last fifteen years. But she was honest enough to know she was justifying. She *did* want to marry and have kids. That had been her dream all of her life, originally a back-seat to career, now front and center in her dreams. A dream that had eluded her so far, and time *was* running out. More and more she thought she would do anything to make that dream come true, so why was she resisting their suggestions? They were only trying to help her get what she wanted.

"The media is full of airbrushed women. Today's men are as demanding as women. They want perfection!" Tiffany went on knowingly.

"Why would I want a guy who demands a perfect

woman?"

"Because that's the only kind there are?" Marti laughed, and everyone but Liz joined in.

That led to another serious silence, everyone but Liz shaking their head in agreement, followed by a chorus of pitying looks in Liz's direction.

Phyllis, the long-suffering one in this group, took Liz's hands in hers and said as if she were talking to one of the kids in the daycare she ran, or to a mental defective, "You have to play it the way they want to play it, Liz. It's pay for play. Once you've got the guy, the kids, the house, car, boat, fabulous clothes and vacations and more, if you get bored, you can let your hair down. By then you'll be tired of him and the divorce won't matter because you'll get half of what he earns anyway and really, that's the whole point in playing the game, get the guy with the most dough."

"That sounds incredibly cynical," Liz weakly told her twice-divorced cousin.

"That sounds realistic," Tiffany said. "There are a million women out there. Three for every guy. It's a box of chocolates and you want them to pick you so you have to be the fanciest, most intriguing truffle in the box."

"Are you *Forest Gump*ing me?"

"Whatever it takes!"

They all nodded, even Marti—her close girlfriend since high school—and Liz felt herself cave.

Marti accompanied her to the dermatologist's office. The wizened man with huge dark eyes behind Coke-bottle glasses was not at all like the *Nip/Tuck* actors in a show she used to watch. Sharp-featured with mud-colored corkscrew hair, olive-complexioned, zero lips to speak of and tiny ears, a face a lower-life-form might admire. He moved furtively,

as if he had ADD. She wondered why, if he was such a renowned dermatologist, he didn't take advantage of his own
skills.

"No good, no good," Doctor Todd mumbled, examining
her skin under a ten times magnifying glass surrounded by
bright LED light that was attached to the reclining clinic
chair positioned to nearly prone.

Besides those few words, he only made sounds, like soft
moans followed by clicks at the end, as if he was in pain. His
breath wasn't the greatest and Liz held hers.

He poked and prodded and stretched the skin on her face
with his fingers and instruments, moaning and clicking
softly all the while.

Marti, who had insisted on coming into the exam room to
hold Liz's hands, said, "She's not too far gone, is she?"

To which *Doctor Doom*, as Liz was now thinking of the
man, moaned and clicked.

Marti patted her hand but Liz couldn't even feel it, she
was so stressed.

Finally, Dr. Todd diagnosed, "Damaged!" in a tone that
conveyed blame. His accent was vaguely New England with
a Germanic twist, and she began to wonder about his history. He was such an odd duck, like something out of a
Grimm's fairytale. "Exposed!" he suddenly snapped, gesturing wildly at her face.

Liz assumed he meant to sunshine. "I, well, a bit, but I
wore sunscreen as a child. Mom always made us wear it."

When he said nothing, she added, "The high SPF type."

He scowled, thin lips turning down, and mumbled dis-
dainfully a word that sounded like *sun* or *shun* or something
she couldn't make out.

"What can you do for her?" Marti asked nervously, as if
Liz had gotten a diagnosis of *terminal*.

"Surgery!" he said unequivocally. "New face." The last

tinged with repugnance.

"No!" Liz shook her head, jerking upright. "Not happening!"

A deeper scowl from Dr. Doom, who looked as if he were about to throw up his hands and order her to 'get out!'

"She's afraid of the knife," Marti supplied.

That wasn't strictly true. Liz had undergone dental surgery once to remove two impacted wisdom teeth. She'd recovered quickly and painlessly. And while she had no desire to repeat the experience, she didn't feel fear so much as the logical reaction: *why do something so extreme? What's the point?* But she did appreciate her friend going to bat for her.

"You mentioned Botox," she said to Marti, who looked hopefully to Dr. Todd.

He gave a quick nod, turning his back on them in dismissal.

"Fills?" Marti asked the back.

He emitted one of those moaning/clicking sounds.

"You need the works," Marti whispered to Liz on their way out of the examination room. "You should have plastic surgery."

"Don't even go there, Marti. I'll do the rest, but not that."

An appointment was arranged for the first of what would turn out to be many regular visits over many months for a variety of treatments, all administered by the strange Dr. Todd who, with the passing of time, in Liz's eyes, had grown a tad less grotesque, not that he was friendlier than the day she'd met him.

She often wondered if it was the intimacy of the procedures he did on her face that changed her perception of him. He had two assistants who performed facials and other minor treatments on patients, but he always worked on Liz himself. She found that oddly comforting. Or maybe he just felt she needed so much help he couldn't trust anyone else to get it right.

Marti had come with her to the first two appointments, after which Liz was on her own. The peculiar man usually eyed her as if she was a bug pinned to a board. Being in his presence made her shudder at times, especially at the beginning, but the procedures were somewhat invasive and she felt that was likely the underpinnings of her fear.

But oddly, after one year of twice a month visits, she realized she did look better and her skin appeared almost new; the sun damage, the acne scars, the rosacea, the premature wrinkles that had become permanent, all of it had vanished. She also felt more comfortable in his presence. He never said *hello*, just nodded, waved at the gown to cover her clothes and at the chair. He still said little more than "Head" with a gesture to turn one way or the other, but somehow he didn't seem as frightening as before.

She told Marti this over coffee at their favorite cafe.

"It's not so bad. I mean, he gives me a shot of something right away, to calm me down, and that really helps. It's as if I daydream and only wake up at the end. I never even feel the needles. The fills, well, I don't feel them in his office, but later I do, for a day or so."

"Yeah, it's a little like having rubber under the skin," Marti agreed. "I always feel as if I'm wearing a mask on the inside of my face."

"Ugh!"

"You look great, though. I mean, twenty years younger! More. My god, I should go to him myself!"

"I wouldn't say twenty. Maybe ten."

"No, at least twenty."

"Well, I've gained a little weight. Maybe ten pounds. Can you tell?"

"Yes. Looks more like twenty."

"Marti, can you be other than honest for once? Jeez. Maybe closer to twenty. Okay, maybe twenty-five!"

"Well, it doesn't look bad on you."

"You told me a year ago to *lose* ten pounds!"

"That was then. The face makes all the difference. So moon-like, vibrant. Your skin looks so . . . healthy! You're like a different person. You know, I hardly recognize you at times. It really is as if you've got an entirely new face."

They paused as the waiter brought their coffees.

"But you're more comfortable with him?" Marti said, opening a packet of sugar substitute and stirring it into her single shot espresso.

"Yes, I am. He's not really friendly, but I appreciate his professionalism."

"You should marry him!"

Liz burned her lip on her latte. "What? Are you out of your mind?"

"He's a doctor. You'd have everything you've ever dreamed of. A husband, kids, a house. Financial security."

"But I'm not attracted to him!"

"You just said you're comfy with him."

"*Comfortable.* In a patient/doctor sense."

"Well, you've spent more time with him than any other man this last year."

Liz knew that was true. Despite all the treatments—and she did look much younger—she hadn't had a date since beginning with Dr. Todd. Of course, she hadn't had a date for half a decade before that either.

To get her friend off the subject, Liz said dismissively, "Marti, I'm sure he's married, so that's that."

"Don't be silly, Liz. Besides, I looked him up in *The American Academy of Dermatology*. There's not a lot of info but he's single, and from meeting him, I didn't see any indications he's gay. You're pushing forty. Go after him!"

Liz was appalled. The idea of a romance with Dr. Doom was absurd. But she put an end to it by saying, "Well, I wouldn't know how even if I was interested, which I'm not."

"Liz, you're so funny! Just be your sweet self. I'm certain he's noticed you by now."

Liz wasn't so sure of that. He was the most aloof man she'd ever encountered. If she'd seen him disembark from a space ship, she wouldn't be surprised."

"Look, here's what you do . . ."

Marti rattled off a list of ways to flirt:

"Smile. Make eye contact and hold it. Flip your hair around and play with your jewelry——"

"Oh, that's ridiculous!"

"Trust me, Liz, men like that, they really do. And it's a signal. And you've got to make sure you run into him outside the office."

"How would I do that?"

"Hide outside and follow him."

"Liz, that's stalking!"

"That's planning. And while we're at it, make sure you dress well. You should *always* look good."

Liz groaned. "This is *sooooo* wrong——"

"Smile a lot. Talk to him——"

"He doesn't say much, you know that, just that weirdness that comes out of his mouth and——"

"And make sure you touch him."

"What? That's assault!"

"Oh, Liz, I mean just touch his arm or something as you say 'Thank you!' Men read that as *she wants me!* And don't forget to smile. It's all pheromones. You put them out, he reacts."

"I'm getting a headache," Liz said. Now she was even more appalled. Had women always done this to get a man? No wonder she was single! What had the world come to?

As if reading her mind, Marti said, "Women have always used tricks like this. Once he's interested, well, marriage is right around the corner."

She paused and looked seriously at Liz. "You, my friend, would be a great candidate for an arranged marriage. Maybe you should visit a professional matchmaker?" Without missing a beat, Marti grinned, "In fact, *I'm* going to arrange things."

A little of the latte Liz held spilled onto the table. "What? No. No! Don't do that, I——"

"I'll have a small dinner party, you and Dr. Toddy, Tiffany and Jim, me and . . . well, I'll find someone."

"Marti, please, don't——"

Marti grabbed her free hand and said, "Lizzy, give it a chance, okay? See the man in a social setting, outside work. He's probably a very nice guy when he drops the professionalism. Cut him some slack."

A week later Liz reluctantly showed up at Marti's apartment, tightly clutching the neck of a bottle of Chardonnay. Tiffany and Jim had already arrived, and Marti's gay friend Andy was there, but no Dr. Todd.

Fear knotting her stomach, Liz rushed to the kitchen to chill the wine in the refrigerator and try to calm down, but Marti followed her.

"Don't worry, he'll be here," Marti whispered, hugging Liz.

"I'm not worried, I'm *relieved* he's not here."

Suddenly the doorbell rang. "See?" Marti said, giving her another small hug and a wink, and went to answer.

Liz hugged herself and chewed the lipstick off her lower lip. This was such a *very* bad idea. Dr. Todd was not her type at all, although Marti, Tiffany and Phyllis—even her mother when Liz had petitioned her—had all assured her she *had* no type. "Bottom line," Phyllis said, "you can grow to love any man. At least for a while." But Liz didn't think she could ever love Dr. Todd—what the hell was his first name, or was that it?

She heard Marti introducing him to everyone, then she heard her say, "Oh, come with me. Liz is in the kitchen."

Good God! Liz thought. Panicked, she glanced around, even though she knew there was only one door, no other exit.

Dr. Todd appeared in that doorway behind Marti, at least a head shorter than her friend who was the same height as Liz. He stood as if frozen to the spot and just stared at her while Marti chatted away. *Maybe he didn't know I'd be here,* Liz thought, *and this is as awkward and embarrassing and such an obvious setup to him as it is to me.*

"Hello, Dr. Todd," she finally stammered, trying to be gracious.

He gave a perfunctory nod.

"I'll be right back, you two!" Marti chirped, leaving them alone in the kitchen.

Panic rose tsunami-like within her and Liz side-stepped it and plunged into pseudo hostess mode. She convinced herself that he was uncomfortable. Even if he wasn't, *she* was.

"It was nice of you to accept Marti's invitation."

His eyes examined her face as they did in the treatment room, the look a bit more pleasant than any she'd seen him provide before. *He's assessing his work,* she thought, disappointed. Even though she wasn't interested in him, still, she had feelings and wanted to be seen as an attractive woman, a desirable person, not as a clinical study. It made her a bit gruff.

"Would you like some wine?" she asked, turning abruptly to the fridge and retrieving the still-warm white wine.

When he didn't answer, she found a corkscrew in the kitchen-implement's drawer and opened the bottle, reached for a glass and then, on impulse, took a second glass and poured wine into both. She picked up the glasses, turned and handed one to him.

At first he didn't take it, as if he didn't know what to do with it, but then he reached out and their fingers brushed. His were cool. She sipped the wine from her glass and he watched her as if she were enacting a ritual, which he then imitated.

Liz took a very large swallow of wine and he imitated that as well. Then she finished off the glass, and, after he'd done the same, she burst out laughing.

"Dr. Todd, you're a strange man," she said, pouring them both more wine.

"There you are!" Tiffany chirped, entering the kitchen. "Just grabbing the Riesling," she sang, squiggling her way between them to the fridge. "Jim's favorite. Then I'll leave you two alone."

"We're just heading in to the living room," Liz said, moving past Tiffany and, maybe the wine was getting to her, grabbing Dr. Todd by the hand and pulling him along.

They sat on one of the two couches across from Marti and Andy. Tiffany and Jim had the loveseat. The cream-colored seating surrounded the large glass-and-brass coffee table. The rest of the evening was sometimes pleasant, sometimes awkward chit-chat but, other than that, uneventful. Everyone talked and laughed and joked and ate, everyone but Dr. Todd. He barely responded to the questions they asked, trying to draw him out. He did, though, drink more wine. Liz realized that he was still imitating her, at least with drinking, and she made sure to ply herself with enough *vin* to feel no pain, and hoped Dr. Toddy, as Marti called him, was doing the same.

Tiffany and Jim escaped after dinner with the excuse to 'see about the kids'. Marti's friend Andy departed. Marti gave Liz a look, yawned and finally said, "I should get my beauty sleep. Tomorrow's a big day at the office."

Liz stood immediately and again Dr. Todd imitated her. He followed her to the door and after Liz and Marti said goodbye and Marti thanked Dr. Todd for coming and he only nodded, Liz led him downstairs.

There were only two cars left in the visitors' parking lot. The green Toyota was hers, the metallic brown Lexus must be his. They got to the Lexus first.

"Well, it's been a pleasure seeing you outside your office," she said with a smile, flipping her hair, wondering if using the word *pleasure* was laying it on too thick. A small moan and click escaped his lips. He scanned her face again and she imagined he was looking for imperfections. As she turned towards her car, slightly off balance from all the wine, suddenly Liz felt something pinch her neck. Her hand went to the spot as instantly she became dizzy and stumbled. "What the . . .?" The parking lot came up to meet her.

When Liz woke, she had no idea where she was. Not her apartment, that was for sure. Not even a house. More like a medical clinic, a white-walled, stainless-steel room devoid of color. She lay on a gurney and soon pulled herself to a seated position too fast; her head swam.

Once she'd gained control of her brain, she glanced around. This looked like an operating room! Many pieces of equipment were familiar and replicated those in Dr. Todd's office. She was dressed in only a hospital gown the color of dirt.

One wall held a windowless door and gradually she eased off the gurney and stood, holding on for support. The room was cool, the stainless-steel cold on her fingers, the floor icy against the soles of her feet. She grabbed the thin brown blanket at the foot of the bed and wrapped it around her shoulders. Despite feeling empty-headed, Liz forced herself to move to the door, expecting it to be locked, but it was not.

She felt weak but not about to faint. If anything, she was confused, not sure how she'd gotten to what was apparently a medical facility of some sort, not knowing what was the matter with her.

She wandered down a short hallway and headed towards a door at the far end. Halfway there, she came to a window and gasped at her reflection. Fear surged and a hand flew to her forehead. Only her eyes, nostrils and lips were visible; the rest of her head was bandaged. "What happened to me?" she whispered. Could she have been in an accident? Many questions, no answers, no memory of how she'd gotten here and into this state.

As the panic cranked down a notch, her eyes refocused and she saw the room within. It was a nursery, full of incubators, three of which formed a circle in the center of the room. Each held a newborn wrapped in a pink or blue baby blanket, hooked up with many tubes to various equipment some of which she could identify, like the blood pressure monitors and the respirators. She had no idea what was going on but instinctively opened the door next to the window and went in.

She moved into the middle of the circle, surrounded by the three incubators. Each of these infants was extremely tiny, more so than the newborns she'd seen, like Tiffany's four. These babies were easily one quarter their size, and swaddled completely so that even their faces were covered, as if they needed exceptional warmth in this dimly-lit room. She guessed these were preemies, hooked up by many tubes and wires to the machinery keeping them alive until they could mature enough to survive on their own. *Whose babies are these?* she wondered. She glanced around but there didn't seem to be any cameras monitoring these little ones, as if they'd been left to their own devices, as she had been.

She reached through the incubator's sleeve to one of the babies and her hand slid into the latex glove at the other end. For some reason, she just had to see what they looked like. Gingerly, she unwrapped the blanket from the face.

And jerked her hand away with a gasp! "No! This can't be!"

Quickly she unwrapped the faces of the other two infants. They were identical, their features distinct even at what must be just days maybe only hours of life. Every one resembled Dr. Todd! Except for one thing: the antennae. The mechanoreceptors at the tips were all turned towards *her!*

This is insane! she thought. Her mind couldn't grasp it. What were these insectoid creatures? She found a chair by the door and sat trembling, struggling to get her bearings. And suddenly realized that her body was different. She was much lighter, as if she had lost a lot of weight. She pressed the gown against her stomach—it flattened! The thirty pounds she'd gained over the last year were gone!

Realization of the more than possible, the *probable* crashed over her. She worked with insects and knew quite a bit about them. *Viviparous* roaches grow their eggs within the *ootheca* sac inside the uterus of the mother, surrounded by fluid. Just like mammals! And they recognize their mother. These were *her* babies and they had recognized her! And now she knew why she had never been conscious during the treatments with Dr. Todd. He'd given her a knock-out drug and raped her. Probably many times.

Revulsion overtook her and she bent to vomit but the heaving was dry, bringing up nothing, and finally she pulled herself up and sucked in air to get control. Either she was crazy and imagining all this, or it had happened, and the reality before her felt ultra-real.

In a panic, she peered again at her reflection in the window. Terrified but determined, she unwrapped the bandage covering her head. With quivering fingers, she peeled away layers of gauze until she reached the final layer. Even before she removed it, she could see that her face was different now, not the smooth, even lines that had been sculpted and shaped by Dr. Todd over twelve months. And the color beneath the gauze was two-toned, pale and dark.

Liz took a deep, rattled breath; she had to know.

She unwound the last layer of bandage and screamed, waking the babies, who also screamed. "My face! My face!" Behind her, Dr. Todd's image appeared, so like those babies, so insectoid.

She spun around, shrieking, "What have you done?"

Expressionless as always, he seemed unperturbed. A little moan. A small click. His almost non-existent lips might have turned up in a smile and released a word that sounded like "Beautiful!"

"What have you done to my face?" she screamed.

He gestured towards the babies. She shook her head, confused, unable to comprehend the incomprehensible.

"Food," he moaned matter-of-factly, clicking insect-like.

"Food," she repeated dumbly. And then understood why he'd created the 'normal' face—one that did not disgust him as much, one rich in healthy, youthful, nutritious tissue. Why he'd brought her to his lair to give birth to his spawn. Why he'd stripped away pieces of that normal mask she'd worn for the last year and left this face with patches of skin removed.

Horror descended on her and she thought she would faint but instead found the path to madness welcoming and headed rapidly down it. Dr. Todd gripped her arm and led her back to the incubators.

"Hungry," he said, moaning, clicking, gesturing towards

the hideous, screaming things in the incubators, their antenna waving frantically in her direction. His offspring. Her offspring. Insects with human features.

He used a tweezer-like instrument to pull a new strip of flesh from her cheek, and she did not feel any pain; she felt nothing. He shredded it into three small parts and began feeding the first of the demon newborns.

Liz watches the infants consume a part of her, watches from this new, safe place within her, abstractly fascinated, buried beneath a core shock from which she knows she is irretrievable. She recognizes that he is an entirely different species, ancient, one predating human existence, perhaps otherworldly. A creature devoid of human emotions and concerns, that has evolved to live among us, breeding with pheromone-producing human females in order to survive. But to what end?

As she stares at the tiny beings devouring her skin she numbly wonders, *Will they eat just this perfect face he's created or will they also demand the less-than-perfect flesh from my body? Does it matter?*

As Marti predicted, Liz now has everything she's wanted—a husband, children . . . *This must be the good life,* she thinks. A life that will no doubt be short.

Tiffany was right after all. Like females, males of every species know what they want. At last, she is perfect in someone's eyes.

Cousin Phyllis had said, 'You can grow to love any man. At least for a while.' *Even a man who is not a man?*

She takes the last strip of her skin from his twitchy hand. "I'll do it," she says, and begins to feed her smallest daughter, whose antennae wave longingly in her direction.

Flesh and Bones

"We need to experience this! *Nous avons de l'argent à faire un don.*"

Joe thought that the old priest closing the door for the day must have heard the supplicant in Marielle's tone. Or noticed the obsessive flicker in her eyes. Or understood the offer of payment. But possibly, it was simply religious compassion that compelled the man to open wide the huge wooden door and say something in Italian that neither Joe nor Marielle could decipher.

Marielle was closest, Joe right behind her, his body pressed lightly up against her too-warm flesh until they followed the priest in, trailed by a small group of five that had gathered, configurations of tourists who also demanded entrance to Rome's Capuchin Church of the Immaculate Conception. Or, more specifically, to its bowels, the Capuchin Crypt.

The black-robed priest stepped aside and they entered, congregating just inside the door, waiting for him to move his hunched body to the table and sit so that he could collect a few Euros from each visitor. Pamphlets were available on a rack for those who wanted them, and Joe snagged two, one in English for himself, one for Marielle in French, a Euro each. Individually and in couples they all went down the half dozen stone steps and then started along the corridor that Joe estimated to be about sixty feet in length, with six 'rooms' on the left side.

This was the most recent crypt on their itinerary, a tour

that had Joe and Marielle travelling from their home in Montréal to various places around the world to investigate human remains in the form of bones (her) and mummified flesh (him). Over the last twenty years, since they'd met and married, they had travelled as often as they could, every year on a four-to-six-week holiday, searching out exotic and macabre locations. This year, Joe's tenure at McGill University allowed for an eight-month sabbatical. Marielle had taken a very early retirement from her senior supervisory position with the Québec government two years before. "I won't live forever," she'd said. "I want to devote my remaining time to my art."

And Joe understood that only too well. Her decision had accelerated his own need. He was as dedicated to mummies as she was to bones. And even after completing ninety-nine percent of this four-month trip through Europe and the United Kingdom at tremendous expense, covering many dozens of bone crypts and mummy museums, neither was ready to go home, although, at the moment, Marielle's pet project called more loudly to her than did Joe's to him.

Like all crypts, the lighting here was subdued, funereal, the occasional small vent providing filtered natural light, creating an ambiance that suited the dead. The scent of centuries of dust and old mold permeated the cool air mixed with a tinge of the traditional tallow from church candles. And while the others hurried through, surreptitiously snapping photos despite the picture of a camera in a circle with a red slash through it, Joe and Marielle lingered. They took photos also, but with the spy cameras each had acquired, two by two inches, Marielle's on a key ring, Joe's disguised as a pen. Years ago, they had realized that too many crypts, ossuaries and museums did not permit photographs. They needed photos, not merely as reminders, or mental *souvenirs* as Marielle called them, and not just to help with their personal projects, but more, to keep their spirits buoyed between trips when they could experience these wondrous remains in person and not just in books and videos on the Internet.

Joe reached the first room on the left. Inside stood a marble altar, a metal cross atop with the usual INRA inscribed over the crucified figure of Christ, and he felt a bit disappointed. Marielle was ahead of him, just passing beneath the corridor's first arched doorway that led to the rest of the rooms. She stopped dead, looked up, then turned to him with awe saturating her features and silently pointed above her head at the ceiling. He stepped aside to let the last of the other tourists pass who were ready to flee what they and most people likely deemed a place too morbid to enjoy. Joe joined Marielle and looked up.

Above their heads hung a large chandelier created from human bones, brown and smooth with age and sprinkled with crypt dust. "Mainly tibia and fibula," she mumbled softly, her voice reverent, "and the tarsals, of course," but Joe heard her.

"That looks like a clavicle at the center," he said, pointing, and she nodded.

Bones were what entranced her. She said now what she had said so often in so many ways, "They reduce us to our essence. It's the bottom line of the physical. After that, there is only *l'esprit, n'est pas?*"

He understood her fascination. He shared it, but not to the same extent. His focus was elsewhere.

He looked ahead, not even glancing towards the second room on the left, wanting to build the tension of his excitement because he knew what was coming. He often thought how this resembled sexual tension, allowing the erotic to expand and rise and finally release, like an orgasm. Yes, it was very much like an orgasm. And he could wait.

He continued along the corridor with Marielle. Unlike *Les Catacombes de Paris*, these bones were not simply piles of femurs and tibia and skulls artistically arranged, but most if not all the bones of the body had been fashioned into shapes, objects. Several hearts lined the corridor wall, composed mainly of carpals and metacarpals, the small bones of the hand that would allow for a rounded shape. The second arch they walked beneath and those ahead were decorated in a kind of filigree pattern with cervical and thoracic vertebrae making for a very pretty and welcoming lace-like design to the entrances.

He still ignored the contents of the rooms for the moment, teasing himself, and headed further up the short corridor until he reached the back wall, admiring the artistry along the way. This wall and the ceiling were crammed with images and he was, as always in places like this, astonished by the number of skulls. A clock had been formed, the frame of cervical, thoracic and lumbar vertebrae and ribs, the Roman numerals employing metatarsals and phalanges of the feet but perhaps also the metacarpals and phalanges of the hands—sometimes these bones looked the same to him, but then, unlike Marielle, he was no *ossa* expert.

Marielle whispered, "Look! *L'Horloge!*" The clock had only one hand, he noticed. And as if reading his mind, as so frequently happened, she said, "Time has neither beginning nor end."

There were flowers, vases, crosses of course, but the most elaborate sculpture was a grim reaper, an entire skeleton, dwarf-size, the skull large, gripping in its bony hands a bone scythe on one side of its body, and a scale in balance on the other.

"Oh!" Marielle cried when she saw it, deeply moved and completely enthralled, and he smiled. He loved her passion for bones. She could be profound in her insights, making connections that he struggled to get to, likely because she could really comprehend how all 206 bones in an adult human body fit together and experienced the beauty of that completeness; this helped him accept his own fixations which, he believed, required much more work to grasp.

Here and there a bone had fallen out of an image from the wall or ceiling in the hallway, never to be replaced but crushed underfoot, and when she noticed, she scanned the dirt floor, finding two pieces of cervical vertebrae and what must be a coccyx. Quickly and surreptitiously, she pocketed these after a glance to make sure the priest was not watching. This was illegal, of course—they often mailed them home disguised in *objets d'art* they purchased—getting human remains through airport security proved nearly impossible. But Marielle needed these for her work. She had bones from around the world, piecing them together carefully, a life's mission, to collect every adult bone and build a composite skeleton, an everyman, well, everywoman—the pelvis she had found was female. He admired her devotion to her craft. His own artwork required little in the way of props, just time and study.

Marielle was so taken with the artwork that she had yet to peer into the rooms built from the foundations of this church. They were alone now, and Joe valued the silence, the priest at the end of the corridor quietly, patiently reading.

He walked back up the corridor slowly, finally allowing himself a quick glance into each room, his heart pounding with excitement. These were three-walled, plus floor and ceiling, open at the front, built of the same dusty grey stone, and dimly lit.

Each arched room presented a kind of tableau created by bones, mostly skulls and crossed-bones—the only ones the early church believed were required for resurrection because, they determined, thinking and emotion were housed in the head, and one only needed the leg bones to stand for ascension.

Joe remembered re-reading on the Internet that morning that monks who had fled the French Revolution in the 1700s had come to join this church, built in 1642, and over the next century and a bit 4,000 of them had died here, their remains contributing to the ghastly decor. The Marquis de Sade had visited this crypt in 1775 and deemed it, "An example of funerary art worthy of an English mind . . .," created "by a German priest who lived in this house." But, in fact, the person or persons who had arranged the contents of this crypt remained unknown, and that suited Joe. He wanted to keep this perfect blend of his and Marielle's interests anonymous.

There were altars, naturally, with crosses above, rounded or squared or rectangular tables and beds, all built from bones. But this is not what caused the adrenalin to rush through Joe's body. What set his heart quivering were those who sat or reclined in or stood near the bed-like niches along the side walls. These stone shelves were the final resting places for the remains of mummified monks, their dark, leathery skin with empty eye sockets and remaining yellowed teeth, the bones of hands and arms and feet extending from the sleeves and hems of the dusty brown robes with hoods they wore and tied at the waist with rough hemp belts. Each exposed face was unique, full of expression, so alive to Joe that he felt they were drawing him closer, wanting him near enough to converse with. He gasped in delight, then quickly looked down the corridor. The priest had looked up.

Joe turned away and took a few steps towards the front of the corridor, gazing at the ceiling, then stopped again, and out of the corner of his eye saw that the priest had returned to his reading.

He turned to the next room, his entrance again blocked by a waist-high fence and, spellbound, stared at the figures, willing them to move, although he knew they could not. He felt an intimacy with the formerly living, *home* for him in a deep sense, and could not tear his eyes from the garbed figures. He wandered back and forth before the rooms, lost in time and space, studying each monk, the supine, the standing, the sitting, their positioning and gestures, memorizing the browned flesh stretched over cheek and jaw and forehead until each face was imprinted in his memory, their hands and feet, their postures, back and forth, identifying every monk in his mind: The Silent One; The Reader; The Heavy One; The Sad Monk; The One Who Could Not Fully Submit . . . until the priest cleared his throat.

"We are nearly finished," Marielle called sweetly, first in English, then French, and if the priest knew either language, he did not let on.

This was Joe's signal to hurry and snap photos, and he removed the pen from his shirt pocket and a small book, pretending to jot notes while he took photos of these beautiful beings.

He exited the crypt with heavy sadness, as if leaving close friends or family that he might never see again. Marielle, by contrast, was happy, talkative, discussing the artistic bone creations, and he found himself tuning her out. It was only later, after a late supper and to bed early because they were headed north to Ferentillo in the morning, that he lay in the quiet darkness apart from her too-warm body, and wondered about why this was so, why this desiccated flesh appealed to him, excited him, made him want to be close, to touch, though he had not often been so close. But one time, in southern Peru. When they had been in the Camarones Valley, he had found part of the face of a Chinchorro mummy that must be 5,000 years old. It was one of the few times he had been up close and personal with a mummy and had felt the parchment-like skin of this ancient being, caressing the millennia-old flesh that ultimately reached the most ancient part of himself, leaving behind the alienated being that took pride of place within him.

The Chinchorra were artificial mummies, the organs removed as with the Egyptian mummies that came 2,000 years later. He preferred the naturally preserved, and knew that the Capuchin monks which he had seen here in *Roma*, as well as those in the enormous and overwhelming *Catacombe dei Cappuccini* in Palermo that housed about 1,000 mummies dating from 1599, both religious and secular, these were all 'natural' mummifications. It was the tuffaceous rock, or porous limestone in the soil which had done the work in nine months, *the time it takes to birth a baby*, he thought.

There were other natural mummies, of course, and he had seen almost all that had been discovered, including the 108 in the *Museo de las Momias* in Guanajuato, Mexico, exhumed from their graves in the adjacent cemetery; the bog people resurrected from the peat bogs of Northern Europe, preserved by the acidic water, low temperature and lack of oxygen; the thirteenth-century Maronite villagers found in a low humidity grotto in the Kadisha Valley, Lebanon, the soil free of decay-causing organisms; the 1000 tombs housing mummies in the Astana graves at Xinijang, China, preserved by the arid air; 'Ötzi,' the 5,300 year old Neolithic mummified man found in the ice-bound Italian Alps and housed at the south Tyrol Museum of Archeology which they had visited just two weeks before . . .

When he thought about it, he became grim with the knowledge that he had now seen every known mummy that it was possible to see, even using his academic credentials to request study of those that were not available to the general public. Ferentillo was their last stop. And then . . . then, what would he do? Go back to his regular life, crammed with students asking questions he had heard a million times, dealing with poorly-thought-out papers, the obligatory wine and cheese *soirées*, the faculty meetings and politics that bored him to death, all of it miring life in mundanity, which he considered worse than death. How could he go back to his 'life'? He *needed* this connection. He could not survive without it.

The following morning they took a train, a bus and then walked two miles through a sun-soaked valley to the sleepy village of Ferentillo and had to wait for the *Chiesa di S. Stefano* to reopen after lunch. They sat in the sun, watching two slow-moving cats meander up the steep path toward where they sat at the church's doorway.

"You seem pensive," Marielle said, petting one of the cats. "Do you regret going home?"

"Yes. Don't you?"

"Not so much this time. I have what I need."

Joe knew she was referring to the bones she had found on this trip, enough to complete her project. He, though, did not share her sense of completion. For him, the mummies would always be elsewhere, never with him, where he needed and wanted them to be. And now that he was about to have seen them all, he felt at a loss.

Marielle reached over and placed her hand on his. "Today is a special day, *mon cher*," she said. "You are finished, too, *non?*"

He said nothing. What was there to say? She was right; his quest, as much as hers, was over. He felt emptiness swell within him that until now he had been able to keep at bay.

Once the crypt beneath the church reopened and they were inside, Marielle immediately headed to a small back room and listened to the caretaker talk about how the mummies and particularly the shelves of skulls had been found. This crypt had only been partially excavated, and there was much more work to do, digging back into the rock to find what could be fifty times as many mummies, but there were no plans in the near future for that work.

Joe only half listened until the caretaker said, ". . . mushrooms in the soil preserved them . . ." This is what he already knew, what, here in Italy, seemed to have been responsible for most of the natural mummification.

He wandered the main crypt area, only a half dozen tall glass and wood cases, one or more mummies within each, dressed, undressed, the sheets of glass keeping them temperature controlled, keeping him from them.

He studied a mummy family, man, woman, infant. Then what might have been a field worker, shreds of a shirt and cap still adhering to the body. A young couple were preserved side by side, her long braided hair hanging over one shoulder the way Marielle sometimes fixed hers. These mummies were pale in comparison to those in *Roma*, their features closer to what they would have looked like alive, and he presumed that the soil which had created the conditions for preservation were responsible for this.

Since arriving in Italy and discovering that the soil combined with various fungi had been the source of drying out a human body in as short a time as four months, his ideas for his own project had shifted 180 degrees. He wanted to explore the possibilities of this fungal soil and consequently touted his academic credentials to allow for the collection of samples he could send home from various locations, where permitted. Unlike the Capuchins in *Roma* and Palermo, here he received permission to collect soil samples for study, which is what he now did. He opened his metallic samples case and filled two dozen large wide-mouthed Teflon-coated glass containers with the dirt by the stone wall at the back of this crypt, what would be less contaminated by human presence, although not many visitors made it to this hard-to-reach town. In Palermo, he had taken soil samples from inside a well near the crypt. The oldest mummy, an early Capuchin monk, had died in a well. His disinterred remains had mummified and Joe had been privileged to view Brother Silvestro.

When he and Marielle were finished with the crypt, they headed back to *Roma* for their flight home the following day. Joe thought about all the places he had been, the mummies he had seen, and the scope and breadth of memory filled the emptiness within, at least temporarily. If only he could hold onto that feeling! If only his life could brim with mummies and the connection he felt to these beings, so real to him, alive to his senses, his way of thinking, connected to his soul . . . If only . . .

Montréal winter met their arrival home. Joe thought that this frigid cold must be similar to what had preserved Ötzi in the Alps for millennia.

But their apartment was comforting, overflowing with sculptures Marielle had constructed, early ones created from animal bones. Since her retirement, the artwork was formed exclusively from human bones she had rescued everywhere they travelled. The Sedlec Ossuary in *Kutná Hora* near Prague had supplied a few. Many were from odd cemeteries, like *Cimetière Notre-Dame-de-Belmont* in Québec City which has a junkyard adjacent where workers tossed old gravestones, coffin pieces and human remains from abandoned graves so the plots could be reused. Once Marielle had crawled into a dumpster against the fence of the Lafayette Cemetery in New Orleans and managed to smuggle home the bones she found there inside voodoo dolls. "So much for perpetual care!" she'd said, but these were all terrific finds that bumped up her work several notches.

Joe had no material from a mummy other than the four-inch square of skin he had smuggled out of Peru. But he did have soil, collected everywhere, searching always for that elusive combination of ingredients that caused natural mummification.

He experimented on dead birds he found in parks, mainly pigeons, and occasionally a larger animal, like a cat. Once he'd come across a dog that had been hit by a car. The soil from Italy showed more promise and over the months of the cold weather, in his climate-controlled lab at the back of the apartment, he had managed to mummify a dead mouse.

During those same frozen months, Marielle finished her sculpture, the 206 bones threaded with forty-gauge wire, thin enough to appear invisible, creating a strangely disjointed figure but lovely in its own right, perpetually in motion, and Marielle was ecstatic. Weeping, she admitted, "I have not the words in any language, *mon amour*. I feel my life is now complete."

Joe debated what to do to move his own project along. He knew what he *wanted* to do, but the climate outside his special room did not inspire this, at least not yet. And like the weather, preservation could not be hurried.

On a day after Winter had given way to Spring and Summer felt within reach, Marielle's spirit seemed to wither before his eyes. She was even more of an introvert than he, and spent hours alone with *La Femme*, as she called the skeleton she had constructed, whispering to her creation.

Her depression deepened until physical symptoms appeared. "Should you see someone?" he asked, but she did not trust doctors and he knew what her answer would be.

"I will drink my *tisane*."

He made her pots of tea throughout the day, the herbs she had drunk all her life, declaring that they would cure anything. But this time, they did not.

"Do not worry, Joseph. Life ends for us all, and I know my time is near. I wish to die as I have lived. You know that, you know me, and you will respect my wishes?"

"Yes, of course," he assured her, and did not argue about it; they had discussed their plans so many times. Joe believed that they had been fortunate to find one another; their passions dovetailed. And while he felt closer to Marielle than to any other living being, still, he felt closer to the preserved dead. He caressed her face, a face he had known and loved for twenty years. Her skin was sallow and dry, the fat and muscle beneath shrunken, and he did not mind this at all, it reminded him of the mummies, and he wished he did not but he preferred her this way.

At the end, Marielle suffered to some extent, but there were drugs for pain relief that he had gotten from his doctor ostensibly for himself, but really for her, and without asking, he crushed the precious blue pills into the tea she drank religiously but eventually could barely swallow.

Joe sat with her, her skin parchment, her eyes, when they opened, glitteringly bright, though sunk into the hollows of her eye sockets. "Remember your promise," she whispered.

She stared at him until he nodded, gently squeezing her arid hand, then her eyes closed, her lips parted, and a sigh like a spirit left her body.

That night, Joe drove to the *Cimetière Notre-Dame-des-Neiges*, to the isolated crypt they had built together a dozen years ago, a small affair, nothing like the elaborate houses of the dead that had been constructed amidst the common graves a century or more ago, or the modern monoliths lacking grace and beauty. Theirs was only wide enough to house two coffins, side by side, with a narrow passage between and a door not four feet from the foot end.

Joe carried her in, her body paper light, naked, washed at home, brought here to her final resting place, and laid her in the open coffin devoid of silks and satins and fancy pillows for the dead. These two caskets were plain affairs, built by Joe of local hardwood, made to measure in length and width, only deep enough so the lids could close if need be.

Rigor mortis had claimed her and while it would pass in a few hours, he wanted to position her right away and struggled with the locked muscles until he was satisfied. Then he sat on the edge of the other coffin, the one measured for his body, touching her now cool skin.

"Forgive me, Marielle. I know this is not everything you requested. You wanted to be interred here without embalming, and I've done that for you. You wanted your body to decompose over time until only your bones are left." He paused. "I'm sorry."

He had placed her on soil he'd collected from around the world and now emptied buckets of tuffaceous fungal dirt on top of her, submerging her limbs, her torso, surrounding her head, leaving only one hand and her moon face exposed, reminding him of the hooded Capuchin mummies.

Finally, he left her to do the things he needed to do to finish up a life. Joe had a sister out west that he hadn't had contact with in over a decade. Unlike him, Marielle had no living relatives and, being a hermit by nature, no close friends. Her pension, as with his salary, was a direct deposit into their bank account, bills paid automatically. The condo ran on its own steam and the neighbors, well, they hardly saw them and rarely spoke.

As he returned the rental car, he thought that with some luck, no one would think to check the crypt.

Two months! he mused, taking the bus in the middle of the night, climbing the cemetery's fence, moving in his dark clothing through these moonless grounds towards the crypt backed up against the forest which he unlocked, entered and relocked from inside. *Not much time for preservation.* He had brought a single candle which he lit and glued with candle wax to the top of the skull of *La Femme,* which now stood undulating in the corner as if guarding her creator.

He so wanted to move the soil away and examine Marielle's body, but that made no sense. A little more than a week wasn't enough time for the drying process to get underway. It would take the full two months of a sweltering summer, and he just hoped there would be an Indian summer this year, extended heat. All the elements were right—the heat, the soil, the fungus—but the time was so short! Well, there was nothing much he could do about that.

Her face looked excruciatingly sweet to him, even more shrunken, skin stretching tight across facial bones already. There was a noxious odor of the gases and other excretions of death but he didn't mind because it would eventually evaporate and the end result was what mattered.

He covered her face with half of the remaining fungus-imbedded soil he had brought here when he'd had the car and had also created the bed of soil in both coffins. Then he undressed and lay in his casket, strapping down his ankles, thighs, stomach, and one wrist.

It was cooler in the crypt but still hot from the day's blazing sun and humidity. Thirty or more Celsius in the day, twenty-eight at night. Not the dry heat of Italy, but maybe it would be all right. He swallowed most of the water in the large water bottle he'd brought along then took her marble-like hand in his and thought about the process.

Over the last days of Marielle's life, he had fed her tea

which contained half a cap of *Aminita bisporigera*—Destroying Angel—a poisonous mushroom which grew abundantly in the forest behind their crypt. This small amount had caused pain but did its work quickly on an immune system defeated; a body with his constitution would suffer much longer and the effects would be more extreme. That's why he had eaten a cap and also dosed his water with two caps, chopped fine in the blender until they were miniscule grains containing the amatoxins. He could already feel the poisonous effects.

"I'm sorry," he said to her again, "but I need you . . . this way."

Before he lost the ability to act, he needed to spread the remaining fungal soil from Ferentillo over his body and face. He reached down between the coffins for the container, and accidently knocked it over!

Powerful stomach cramps hit and he knew vomiting and diarrhea would follow quickly; delirium was creeping through his mind. Horrified, he no longer possessed the strength and coordination to free himself and re-collect the soil. All he could manage was to tightened the strap holding his neck in place, sensing the convulsions about to begin. He again reached for her hand, caressing the cool, dry skin, intertwining their fingers, struggling for consciousness amidst the sharp agony racking his body, suddenly shocked by the clear thought: this would not, *could* not work!

"Flesh and bones!" he cried. *She* would be the flesh, but *he* would become bones!

Tears streamed from his eyes that he did not understand. But one thing he was certain of: he had never felt so close to her.

Gurrl UnDeleted

Esmerelda checked her ticket again. First class, car 2, cabin 3—this must be the right place.

She stepped aside to let a young man pass by then opened the wooden door and entered the small compartment. The sallow-skinned passengers taking up five of the six seats on two facing benches all wore funereal inky black, head to toe, and looked up at her as one unit with suspicion-laced eyes. Two women, three men, not one of them smiling and none potentially friendly. She felt disconcerted and gave them a smile and a "Hello!" anyway, which was ignored. What appeared to be a mother and grown daughter, both with pointy-chinned witch-like crinkly faces and dark beady eyes, turned their heads as if insulted. The bent-over old man may or may not have nodded, but she noticed his head continued to bob so maybe it wasn't a nod. One middle-aged man grunted, and the younger-looking of the two men, still middle-aged, leered, ogling her head to toe, his eyes finally resting at the general area of her breasts.

Oh my God! she thought, folding her arms across her chest, checking her ticket again, and then ducking her head out to verify the number in brass on the door. Not a warm welcome, not a pleasant group; Esme felt intimidated, to put it mildly.

She looked at the luggage racks above the seats on both sides; they were crammed to overflowing with plastic and ugly stripped cloth bags, beat up paper shopping bags, small stained boxes, a filthy backpack. The floor was crowded with more of the same plus little cases and large suitcases, folded garment bags that had seen better days, and even an open shopping buggy. And an empty bird cage, the paper at the bottom littered with spent seed casings and bird shit. It was as if these people were carting everything they owned with them. Which meant she would have to keep her suitcase just in front of or behind her legs so she wouldn't be able to sit comfortably, and it was going to be a long train ride up into the south west of Germany to the Black Forest, then further north up the river Rhine, full of castles, some 1,000 years old!

She took the only space available, next to the two women, who moved as far away from her as they could, as if she had a disease or something, the older one sniffing loudly as if Esme had BO!

Esme stole a fast glance past them out the window. The train had just pulled out of the station and she checked her cell phone; they were on time. That was good. The cell phone message said no reception. Not good.

A sudden smell of decay hit, an undercurrent on the air, and she wondered what was in the process of rotting and figured it was in one of those bags or boxes. Maybe that's what the woman had smelled.

Within one minute a painfully thin, grim-faced conductor with bulging blue eyes and a large nose sporting a giant wart on the tip opened the door to collect tickets. His uniform was wrinkled and had grease spots here and there, his tie askew, as if he'd just gotten out of bed. He reached out a skeletal hand and Esme handed hers over, which he punched, then handed back, giving her a critical frown, his breath reeking of garlic and stale beer.

Suddenly, the black-clad passengers became animated and vocal in a language she had never heard, frantically rooting through bags and boxes, searching for their tickets.

Esme sighed. She thought she'd been oh-so-clever relying

on the advice of the born-yesterday travel agent to go first class instead of getting one of the small rooms or even a berth. "The train is never full, almost empty. You'll probably have the compartment to yourself," the girl had erroneously predicted. A shared cabin in first was cheaper than the berth and certainly much less expensive than a private room, and was supposed to be more comfortable than 2nd class and of course "draws a better crowd," she'd chirped, since it was twice the price of second class. But this hot, cramped space with these strange passengers who looked as if they couldn't even afford space in the baggage car proved to be anything but what Esme expected.

One of the men collected tickets from the others and handed them to the conductor, who didn't seem to notice they were smudged and sticky. He used his hole punch then handed back the tickets.

Once the ticket collector had gone, the train picked up speed. Her compartment mates suddenly began talking, all at once, loudly, babbling over each other, nobody, apparently, listening. She didn't have a clue what language they spoke but she knew it wasn't German or French and didn't sound like Spanish or Italian. Maybe it was a Slavic tongue. There were so many languages in Europe and everyone seemed to speak a smattering of a lot of them. It made her feel stupid and uneducated but where she came from, if you spoke ten words of Spanish, you were considered cosmopolitan.

These words were clicks, like sounds some birds make, and the closest language she remembered hearing with clicking sounds was an Inuit dialect that she'd run across in a National Geographic TV docu. But these people clearly weren't Inuit. Their ragged clothing was a cross between Bedouins, Hassidim, Mennonites with a little Kabuki style tossed in for good measure. But they didn't strike her as part of any known culture.

Soon the witchy women busied themselves with pulling out of the bags strong-smelling food items, a variety of sausages and cheeses, loaves of bread, and bottles of wine that one man opened using a knife to spear the corks and yank them out. The men grabbed the food as soon as it was in sight, like they were starving, tearing into it with their yellow, rotting teeth like ogres, everyone taking bites out of the garlicky meat and hard round bread and the chunks of smelly cheese, passing the food between them in a rapid-motion haphazard pattern, the whole crew digging in. All the while with full mouths they talked non-stop, the volume growing louder, accompanied by wild gesticulating and big slurps of wine directly from the bottles that were also passed around, seemingly not caring that wine dripped down their chins and onto their black costumes. Soon, both the men and the women began belching, but when the two middle-aged men got into a farting contest and stench filled the air, Esme grabbed her suitcase and bolted.

She stood outside the compartment door shaking her head, thinking, *What the hell?* There was no way she'd be sitting in there with them for hours and hours, even if she had to stand in this corridor!

She looked up as a man about her age approached. She thought he was the same guy who had passed her earlier going in the opposite direction. Dark brown hair and eyes, a tan suit, a bit taller than her. *Cute!* she thought, but he didn't even glance her way, just passed on by to the next car towards the front as if she was invisible.

With a sigh, she determined to find the conductor and see what other spaces were available. Even if she ended up in second class for the price of first class, it would be better than that crew.

She headed in the same direction as the cute guy and

found only the conductor in the next car and, grabbing the railing for support, struggled to move on the rocking train dragging her suitcase behind, her purse and heavy laptop straps draped across her chest. These must be the private rooms, a row of nine doors down one side of the aisle, windows with the railing below along the other side of the aisle.

She caught up with the man who had taken the tickets as he exited the last door at the far end. "Uh, excuse me!" she said, but he didn't hear her or was ignoring her, so she touched his arm. He spun around, scowled at her, then glanced down at her suitcase, but didn't say a word.

"I'm wondering," she gave him her most brilliant smile, "if there are any other first class compartments available."

"No." He turned away.

"What about berths?"

"You did not pay for berth," he informed her in broken English.

"Yes, I know. But if there's one available, I'd like to upgrade. I'll pay extra."

"No berths," he said, and walked away.

She yelled after him, "What about a private room?" But he had already moved into the connecting space between cars where the sound of the wheels probably precluded him from hearing her and he was facing away from her anyway, but she saw him shake his head *no* before he disappeared.

"Thanks for your help!" she mumbled.

Esme glanced up then down the empty corridor then threw her free hand into the air and signed. "Great!" she mumbled. "I guess I'm stuck with the sausage eaters!"

Suddenly two very short, serious-looking men came through the door at the other end of the corridor. They were so short and so wide they looked almost square and resembled dwarfs. Skin bronzed by the sun, wearing work shirts and dusty khaki pants and steel-toed work boots, they could have been twins. They both held pails and long-handled brushes and one had a key and opened the door to room number two. When they were both inside, the door slammed closed. She heard the lock turn. They did not look flush enough to afford a private room, but they had one. And she didn't.

Feeling grim, and not yet ready to return to the picnic taking place in what she now thought of as an overpriced first-class prison, she let go of the suitcase handle and grabbed onto the railing with both hands, staring out the window, hoping to catch a glimpse of the land that led to the famous Black Forest, a place that had figured in her fantasies forever. There was nothing to see as the train sped through the night, just her reflection in the glass, ghost-like against the darkness.

She studied that reflection with a critical eye. Twenty-one, tall, attractive enough, she guessed, but no world-class beauty. A touch of frantic around the eyes.

Esme wondered just what it was that had driven her to quit her job spur-of-the-moment. Well, that wasn't true. She had thought about quitting for long enough. Working in gaming as a software designer had been a dream since grade school, but the reality proved to be a nightmare. It sure didn't mesh with her fantasies. Despite the job description, she never got a chance to create unique software, even though she had plenty of ideas for innovative games. But the company just wanted what they wanted, to their specifications, and she was the third level down, so she wasn't even near the creative-concept end of things but stuck at the testing level.

She'd learned early that nobody cared to hear her ideas and, if they did, it was only to steal them, and she felt pretty sure that had happened. She put up with it because this was the best company around by far, the largest, a leader in the gaming world. And when she'd sent out a couple of resumes to other gaming companies, they all wanted to know why she would leave TK-WD. Apparently wanting to leave the highest paying, most glamorous and theoretically most innovative company made her a suspicious potential employee. Either she was trying to infiltrate to steal schematics, or she was stupid and uncreative or a troublemaker or all of the above.

One day, for no particular reason, Jonathan, her direct overlord, stopped by her desk and gave her that smile which she could never figure out, then handed her a memory key and asked her to take it home and "Have a look at this. Tell me what you think." It was probably his current pet project and he wanted to use her expertise to check if there were bugs—like she didn't have enough to do and could use more work at home, especially *his* projects, that would lead to *him* impressing the head honchos and getting yet another promotion while she, the peon who helped him, lingered in the trenches!

"I knew you'd want to check it out," he said with a wink.

Once he was gone, curiosity got the better of her and that afternoon after lunch she slipped the key into her office computer, only to find the specs for a game program for pre-and teen girls that she herself had designed that could, potentially, make the company millions. Her program was on this very computer already, which could only mean that Jonathan had been snooping.

Despair cut into her as if she'd been stabbed in the heart. She folded her arms on her desk and let her head fall onto them, wishing she could just go unconscious, or die, whichever came first, wondering what she could do about this out-and-out theft.

How could Jonathan live with himself? And then she lifted her head and looked around the huge open-concept space filled with desks and state-of-the-art computers and other equipment and at all the tensely-focused low-level techies who did what she did, like her, kidding themselves that one day they would make the leap to the next level, never for a second realizing just how impossible that would be in this world of theft and corruption and nepotism.

She had sat up abruptly, tapped the keyboard rapidly, and deleted all her personal files, then deleted them from the hidden caches and from RAM and ran a virus she'd developed on her own just to screw up this computer permanently, cleaned out her desk, dropped the memory key into the waste basket, set the paper in the basket on fire, and typed the furious giant red letters *I QUIT* onto the screen. Then she walked out the door for good, and to freedom.

And, of course, hadn't been able to get another job. Which is why she decided to take a vacation, since she hadn't ever had one and she'd always wanted to see the Black Forest and she might as well do it now since she had no interviews pending. The least she could do was spend her accumulated vacation pay so she'd feel the entire experience at TK-WD had not been a total loss. And in the back of her mind she entertained the wild hope that maybe a job in Europe would open up. *Or not,* she thought suddenly. She didn't really care. She just looked forward to a relaxing month Elsewhere. Interesting places. New ideas. The unexpected. An experience to refresh her for the battle ahead when she got home and had to face unemployment and her mother's worry-driven chiding and her father's disappointed frowns.

But that was, of course, before the picnickers. Now, she would be stuck in this corridor overnight on this slow-moving train the stupid travel agent described as 'charmingly old-fashioned, quaint'. Surrounded by people who acted like they were in a fairy tale by the Brothers Grimm!

She perched on her suitcase and waited, but for what she

didn't know. For time to elapse, she guessed. She folded her arms across the low railing and put her head down, letting the rocking calm her. It was like being in a cradle, lulled, all the horrors of the real world gone for a while.

"Are you locked out?"

She opened her eyes and turned her head to see the cute guy standing nearby, staring at her, a look of concern on his face.

"Uh, not exactly. More like deleted. Sorry, I mean, displaced."

He smiled a little and finally she added, "I'm supposed to be in a first-class cabin, but the people inside are . . ." she wasn't sure how to say it nicely, "odd. A little too odd."

He smiled, bringing his features to life. "And you're trying to get away from odd."

"Exactly."

"Where are you headed?"

"I want to see the Black Forest. And travel up the Rhine to the castles. I'm on vacation, and these are places I've always wanted to see, because of the Brothers Grimm."

He nodded knowingly. "Both are beautiful," he said. "Magical. The kind of spots where you can get lost, leave your life behind."

"That would be good," she said, "even for a day."

"You know, maybe the conductor can find you another seat."

"I asked. He can't. I guess this train is booked solid."

"That's too bad. There's no dining car or lounge until early tomorrow morning when we reach the Black Forest and change trains." He paused. "I have a private room—this one right here," he said, pointing to door number three. "I don't mind if you want to share it. There are two beds, upper and lower."

She felt wary. Sharing a room with a guy she didn't

know? What kind of craziness was that?

Suddenly he smiled at her again, a disarming smile, one that said he was harmless. "At least come in and sit down for a while so you can get out of the corridor before the cleaning staff comes along and sweeps you away! We can leave the door open. My name's Karl."

That didn't sound risky, so she smiled back and said, "Thanks. Esme. And that would be great."

She stood and grabbed her suitcase handle as he opened the door to a small room with a couch that seated three easily, which probably turned into a bed. Above, there was something in the wall that dropped down which probably became the upper bed. The room was filled with little compartments, all designed for safe storage on a rocking train.

"That's the toilet," he said, pointing to a narrow door.

"Thanks."

She sat by the open corridor door and he took the space by the window, leaving enough room for a person and a half between them. It was awkward but at the same time she felt she should make an effort to be friendly. After all, he had offered her space and she needed that.

"Where are you from?" she asked.

"Here," he opened his arms.

"Oh, you're German. Your English is fantastic."

He smiled. "I speak many languages. And you?"

"The United States. I live in Chicago now but I might be moving somewhere else, once I find a new job."

"What kind of work do you do?"

It wasn't exactly true, since she hadn't yet done that for anyone, but she said, "I design computer games."

"Ah, you live in fantasy."

She laughed. "A bit, I guess. I mean, most of the games I'm interested in designing are weird worlds, you know, fantastical creatures, a little like fairy tales for modern kids."

He gave her a thin smile and she wondered if he disapproved. A lot of people disapproved of gaming.

To change the focus, she said, "And what do you do?"

"I also work with fantasy. Dark fantasy, I guess you'd call it."

She lifted her eyebrows and jerked her head in an 'and?' gesture.

"I help the lost find their way."

A warning bell went off. She hoped he wasn't some religious nut hoping to make her his next convert.

Esme glanced out the opened door and into the hallway, wondering if maybe she should go back to the first-class cabin. At least she knew what to expect from the sausage eaters.

"I only help people who need help. In your world of modern games, think of me as a wizard."

She laughed. "I guess you see a lot of troubled people."

"I do. More than you can imagine. Many people want to escape their lives. The area we'll be entering soon, the Black Forest, seems to draw them. I guess you'd say I save them from themselves," he laughed.

"Really. That's noble work. It must be fulfilling. Me, I only end up playing with images and scenarios, trying to make them work smoothly and feel exciting and unpredictable."

"You'd be surprised at how unpredictable real life is," he said, "like fairy tales, which have different endings depending on the time, place and the country in which they're told."

He spoke in a way that made her think about how her own life had not gone the path she'd envisioned.

They spent the next couple of hours chit-chatting about movies, music, books, the latest software, never really veering towards the personal.

Finally he said, "You must be getting sleepy. Why don't

I go up there and you can have this bed. Feel free to use the bathroom."

She now felt comfortable with him and thought he was safe enough. And what could happen on a train?

"All right," she said. "I appreciate this. And let me pay for half the room."

"Absolutely not! I don't mind, it's nice to have a companion on this train ride. I'm going to shut the door, if you don't mind."

"Sure," she said, rummaging in her suitcase for a T-shirt and jogging pants instead of her nightgown. She wasn't *that* comfortable with him.

She stepped into the tiny washroom, so small she could barely turn around, but managed to change, brush her teeth, wash her face, comb her hair and apply some makeup. *Okay*, she thought, *he's cute, he's nice, but this is crazy. He's just being friendly.* She dabbed a bit more lip gloss onto her lips.

When she came out of the bathroom, the door to the room was closed. The upper bunk was down and he was lying on it, turned towards the wall, and he'd opened up the lower bunk for her.

She reached back into the bathroom for a tissue to wipe off the lip gloss. *So much for that fantasy*, she thought, climbing into the surprisingly comfortable lower bed. There was a small light at the head of the bed and she shut it. And lay in the darkness rocked by the train until she drifted off.

Suddenly a blast of heart-stopping noise jerked her awake. Metal monsters screeched and slammed into one another. A loud wail filled the night and she braced for an impact. A whoosh, like the air was being sucked out of the room.

She bolted upright, heart thudding, staring around her, not quite sure where she was. It took moments to realize that the train window was open at the top and the sound had been another train speeding by, inches from this one, the unearthly rattle of the two reverbing off one another as they passed at top speed.

She jumped out of bed and looked up but had no sense that her roommate had woken. Then she went to the window and peered out. The full moon let her see that the train was now crossing an old bridge. Out of the corner of her eye she thought she saw something peering up from under the bridge, something troll-like, with a large, distorted head and strangely human-like body. That could not be! She blinked and the image was gone.

The train left the bridge and returned to normal train sounds, wheels on tracks, a steady rocking, all of it lulling her, and eventually she lay down again. Finally, she relaxed enough that the rhythm sent her back to dreamland.

Crash! "No! Don't do that! Don't take that! It's mine!" Double crash. She jerked awake with a gasp to the sound of fighting and bashing against the wall next to her. Yelling. Screaming. It sounded as if a body was continuously being slammed against the wall.

Frightened, Esme sat up and called out to her chamber mate in a whisper, "Karl. Karl!" Nothing.

The fight escalated and it sounded as if someone was being murdered. "Let me go! I promise, I'll give it back!" Bash!

She knew it was the next room with the short, square men. She switched on the light at the head of her bed and tentatively swung her feet to the floor. Once she stood, she turned and looked at the upper bunk. Karl lay on his back obviously asleep and how he could sleep through the racket, she did not know.

Bam! Another bash against the wall. Now the victim was shrieking.

She was afraid but had to do something. She didn't know what she'd do if they were in the corridor. There had to be an emergency button to call for help. To stop the train.

She turned the lock and opened the door slowly. Suddenly it was dead quiet. She poked her head out and looked up and down the corridor, hoping the ticket taker or some staff person would come to check out the commotion. She glanced at the door next to hers, where the noise had come from. No one. Nothing. She waited, then tentatively stepped into the corridor and gingerly walked to the door of room two and placed her ear against it. And heard breathing. Deep, heavy breathing, rasping that sounded like someone calling her name—*Esme!* Someone on the other side had their mouth at the same height as her ear!

Esme jumped back quickly and hurried to her room. Quietly she closed and locked the door, then glanced at her roommate. He had turned his back to the wall. She stared at him and he still seemed dead to the world.

Rattled by the fight next door—did she *really* hear her name?—she crawled back into bed and pulled the covers over her head, trying to decide how much of it she'd imagined.

She lay trembling and it took what felt like hours to calm enough that she could turn out the little light. Finally, she drifted into something resembling sleep, jerking awake with every sound but, eventually, falling into a somnambulance.

A sound woke her that could only be called a low moan, like an animal in pain. She was facing the wall and the sound came from directly behind her, near her head.

Fully awake now, she was aware of something close, the moan intense, otherworldly. Her body shook in terror and she could not bring herself to turn around to face what was there. Then, wet sliminess slid up her back to her shoulder. Tap! Tap! Trying to get her attention. She had to turn. She just had to. And did.

Before her was Karl's face, but dead white, his mouth

open and a mist coming from inside of him filling the room like a fog. His eyes were closed, and then he blinked. Eyes like his were painted onto his eyelids. And suddenly, one of those painted eyes winked.

A scream rose from Esme's gut until she was shrieking, unable to stop herself.

"Hey! It's okay. You dozed off. Had a bad dream."

She blinked and stared at Karl . . . No, Jonathan! She looked around in confusion and fear. She was sitting at her desk, her co-workers standing at theirs, Jonathan bending over her in a solicitous manner. His hand on her shoulder. "You dozed off," he said.

Dazed, she looked up to see Bill, the mailroom guy, tall, gangly, wrinkled clothes, scowling, a wart on his nose. Sonia, the office goth, face anorexically thin, holding half a salami sandwich in her black-nailed hand, the scent meaty and garlicky. Across the room, through the glass partition, two workmen, almost as wide as they were tall, were outside the picture window cleaning the glass.

She glanced at her computer screen, at the program from the key Jonathan had given her. There, on the screen, was a train car, the one she had created, the one Jonathan had stolen from her. "My game . . . ," she managed.

"Yeah, and it's a good one. I did some modifications and wanted you to check them. I think we can work this up and present a proposal together to J.D. What do you say?"

She nodded, unable to talk. Startled. Stunned. Confused by everything that had seemed so real but was obviously not.

As her co-workers got back to work, and familiar noise filled the office.

Jonathan said, "Esme, *Gurrl UnDeleted* is a terrific idea, perfect for the pre-and teen girl market the company is trying to crack. You've got potential."

She managed a smile. "Thanks. Sometimes I forget that."

"Well," he said with a wink, "that's what I'm here for, to save you from yourself."

Mourning People

As Genna parked her car at the edge of town, she asked herself, and not for the first time: *Isn't there some magic formula to 'get over it'?* Why couldn't she be one of those who just compartmentalized in that 1% of the brain that left 99% for living life? She felt cheated that she had never suffered ADD; the ability to concentrate had proven to be a curse rather than a blessing.

The pitted road that led in and out of town was empty, desolate in fact, but then it was late, and the citizens of Innsmouth rarely left their houses at twilight.

Genna hadn't been 'home' in forty years, but nothing, it seemed, had changed. If anything, the decrepit place of her birth was in even worse shape than before. Trash and garbage strewn on the streets, cracked sidewalks, broken windows everywhere, walls spray painted with indecipherable graffiti, boarded up factories, houses blackened by fire, others derelict and choked by yards full of chest-high dried weeds . . .

She passed the grade school where some of the grimmer concepts imbedded within her had been formed. From the looks of it, the red brick chimney must have fallen at least a decade ago, caving in parts of the roof on its way—and no one had bothered to fix it! Were there still children coming here to learn the hideous history of this place? Did anyone *live* here? She saw no lights in any windows. Maybe Innsmouth had turned into a ghost town! But its denizens had always been like this, hiding, secretive, creepy in ways that she only became acutely aware of after she escaped.

Her parents' house sat at the dead end of a short street, isolated, the gables warped from wind and moisture, the porch seriously sagging, wood rotting, paint so peeled and faded that the underlying wood showed through creating an ash-grey exterior. She stopped to examine it, but from afar. Even a hundred yards away she felt the chill. Was that faint, mournful high-pitched wailing coming from the house? It sounded so familiar and the thought occurred to Genna: *that might be my voice!* Life had been crushed here. For that reason alone, she did not want to go inside. But, there was no need to enter; a gauzy death shroud blanketed her memories, one that could be lifted at any moment, the sharpened memories triggered by anything, by nothing.

Innsmouth was an old town, established in the 1600s as a trading port, and her tainted roots went deep. Her family had never kept up the house, and in her lifetime, at least, no one seemed to care about the town's upkeep in general. It had been that way when she was a child—buildings, and people, falling apart before your eyes—right up to her sixteenth birthday when she ran away to the city to carve out a life despite the despair imbedded in her psyche. She had longed to inhale a deep and carefree breath for the first time in her young life, and had.

She turned away from the disturbing squalor, left the car, and headed along the dirt-and-sand-embedded-with-gravel trail that led towards the sea. Footprints of generations of her ancestors were pressed one onto another into this path and as she walked, it felt like stepping on graves.

Coming back had been a torturous decision; thoughts of returning terrified her. But with the death of her mother, she had to return. The funeral—such as it was—took place without her; that, she could not have faced. Without being aware of the time, months went by and there were specific things that needed to be done: items to be given away, household furniture to be disposed of, papers to be found and read and preserved or destroyed, the aftermath of death to be taken care of. And there was no one else. The idea of being the last of her line left Genna hopeful. *At least the madness will end with me*, she thought. She hoped!

But she did not come back for the wrap up of a life. She'd had a company pack up everything that wasn't furniture and send it to her office because she did not want these vestiges of the past infecting her home. She sorted through boxes and crates and locked containers that had to be broken into, the contents not worth finding let alone securing and saving, many items strange, unknowable, some so disgusting or hideous that she used gloves to hold those things that she immediately dumped into trash bags and put out on the curb. She'd sorted, filed and shredding and mailed on items to their ultimate destination, paid taxes, disposed of the land by gifting it to the town to do with as they wished. Everything was done but for one thing, and for that, she had no choice but to return.

The path led towards a cove that caressed the sea. This small portion of beach and water was not barriered by the strange black breakfront that mimicked the main harbor's shoreline. Here, the water was free to come and go, the tides ebb and flow naturally, and it was the only spot where Genna had found fragments of peace and comfort as a girl.

As she climbed the little hill, ahead she saw the coldly blue Atlantic. She had spent many days here surrounded by the dead, sitting and staring at the water, watching the breaking waves shove towards shore, then pull back, dreaming under the hot sun of summer, bundled against the icy winds of winter, enduring the storms of every season when the clouds blackened and thunder surrounded her, sometimes lightning so threateningly near that her body trembled involuntarily from a mild shock.

When she was younger, her mother often found her here, scolding verbally, "Stupid, stupid girl, the ocean is not your friend! *Nothing* here is your friend!" She'd yell at Genna as she dragged her home, "This is a cursed place and ours a cursed existence. Take no comfort here. No comfort!" the words indoors followed by the hairbrush until she was taller than her mother and was punished only once more. But by the time she was old enough to escape physically, her psyche had been contaminated.

Leaving home left her breathless for years, half the time frightened, the other half exhilarated, but it provided a catalyst for insight after the fact. Her mother had been insane with misery, leaking bitterness and hatred into the world, a life wasted, her only joy destroying the lives of others. The woman who gave birth to Genna had never cared for village life, never liked the water, regretted marrying and bearing four children, one of whom had died at birth, two others passing before she did, left with only the troublesome daughter who would not readily obey, who often heard the mumbled words, "It should have been you who died!" In the quiet of the night as she rocked by the fireplace, the woman declared Genna's rarely-home father, "That filthy monster! A god-forsaken demon from a place worse than hell!"

Genna had always found her father frightening. His grotesque features, jerky, inhuman mannerisms, the vileness that seeped from his pores and permeated his every action, every word, a man whose touch left her skin feeling diseased, whose very presence seemed to suck out her will, leaving her depleted and depressed. She avoided him as much as she could. And once she had gotten away from Innsmouth, she wondered if her crazy mother had had a point. And then the accident—or was it an accident?—that crippled him, and her mother had no way out until he died, and by then it was too late.

Genna longed for the city, with its opportunities for education, friends, entertainment. Love. And the metropolis she had chosen offered all of that and more. But like a trickle from a stream, she enjoyed a bare minimum of what was possible.

Even before all the deaths, with her first menstruation, Genna found herself attracted to this small family cemetery at the edge of the high cliff above the salty sea that she had just reached. A rusty twisted coat hanger held the gate precariously closed; she opened it and stepped onto the heavily-sanded soil riddled with sea shell shards that housed her ancestors, her siblings, her father, and now her mother. The bones of grandparents, great grandparents, great great grandparents, aunts and uncles, cousins once, twice, three times removed were all interred in this rural plot. Lucky children that had died of cholera just after they were born. Hoary old men who had outlived their timid and frightened wives by decades to finally succumb after a century of ensuring misery for their offspring. Beastly women and their repugnant children buried together. Unknown relatives who had died old or young or middle-aged, their remains in coffins stacked atop one another because within the cast-iron fencing there was limited land in this prison of demise. Years ago, Genna measured the cemetery and determined the square footage to be 666, and was not surprised.

All totaled, just twenty-five headstones crammed the tight bone yard. Made of local stone, several names had been carved on each, the oldest and largest curving gently as befitted grave markers of another age, the more recent deaths inscribed on rectangles the size of a laptop computer. Long before Genna's birth, the windy sea had eroded the earliest names and dates so there was no way to determine the total number of dead.

Her mother hated the cemetery. "Only a ghoul would want to go there!" she had shouted, her tone rising to the familiar shriek. "Wicked, you were born bad, of your father's side!"

"My morbid one," her father dubbed her in his monotonous tone, catching her arm with his icy hand, pulling her close, breathing his rank, stale breath of mold and rot into her ear like a worm crawling into the canal, infecting her brain. Words that might, from less of an alien being, have been an endearment. But from him they were tainted by the inhuman look in his rheumy eyes that spoke of dangerous realms where death and madness ruled. Had he been afraid *of* her or afraid *for* her? More likely, he was not afraid at all.

And now her mother lay buried in this stifling seaside cemetery, a place in which Genna had no intention of spending eternity, crushed between an unforgiving mother, a fiend of a father, dead siblings, and surrounded and suffocated by the negativity and hopelessness and pure evil of this long line of rotting corpses. As she stood over the marker already inscribed with her mother's dates, she was well aware of her own name chiseled into the rock—date of birth, no date of death. Yet.

"No way!" she snapped. Genna had already made her wishes known, written a Will, prepaid funeral arrangements, bought a space for a cremation urn in a cemetery far from here, leaving whatever money she had to charity.

She turned away from the markers of death and walked to the south eastern corner of the cemetery fence which overlooked the edge of the bluff, her eyes taking in the vast and relatively quiet sea beyond. The tide was in, the water very high up the cliff wall, and she knew it would only take one good storm at high tide for strong waves to overtake the sandy ground, flood the cemetery, and wash away graves.

That had happened in the past, many times it was said, but apparently no waves had been powerful enough to completely decimate this little village of the dead. Genna hoped that would change. She would like nothing better than to see this testament to a ghastly family from a malevolent town in a world that was increasingly proving itself insane washed away forever. "Let the dead die!" she mumbled.

Suddenly, a wave crashed over the edge of the cliff, nearly knocking her off her feet, soaking her and the burial grounds. Startled, Genna braced for another onslaught. But the ocean regained its composure. For now. If there was one thing she had learned as a girl it was that the sea was mercurial—anything could happen at any moment and, like everyone in her family, the ocean could be merciless.

The south western corner had not been drenched by the wave and she walked there to the little park-bench-like chair for one that she had sat in as a girl, the wood extremely weathered, the metal arms and legs rusted. She had loved to sit here facing the many dozens of enormous sandstone spires that had formed over the millennia, just beyond her reach.

Had they changed in four decades? She sat down and began to count them as she had done as a child, then stopped herself from enacting this useless ritual. Oddly, every death in her family produced a new limestone stack, or that's what she thought when she was young and then later rationalized that she had miscounted, though she was not convinced that she had. These 'people' as she liked to think of them, were a curiosity. A fluke of nature. There had been no one to ask about this—certainly not her parents. After she left home she had done research on this phenomenon, but nothing she read explained why or how new spires could form so quickly. Like so many things in her life, she could only attribute this weirdness to the town itself. Her mother had been right about one thing: Innsmouth *was* cursed.

She threw back her head and looked up: the hardened conicals stretched higher than the burial grounds, higher than the town itself. Their pointed tips resembled fangs hellbent on piercing the darkening sky, ten, twenty, fifty feet above the cliff, like children, women and men, tapering, and at the top a small head-like ball had formed. As a child she had talked to her 'people', but they never answered. That was probably just as well.

"You've been silent all this time," she said now, and the towers said nothing. "Are you guardians? Watching over the graves? One for each of them, like sentinels, protecting from above the monsters that lie below? Or are you protecting me from the monsters? What are you?"

The morning of her sixteenth birthday, at low tide, she had descended the cliff and spent the day wandering the beach between these enormous pillars, stepping carefully over the jagged rocks connecting them. She touched every one, their porous surfaces like rough skin, mica sparkling jewel-like in the sun. That day, she became mesmerized by these ancient spires, connected to these 'people' individually and as a 'family'—and she lost track of time.

As the tide rolled in, water washed up to her ankles, then to her knees, hips, waist, up to her chest, chilling her skin and muscle and to the bone, until she shivered uncontrollably. "I could die here," she told the spires, hoping that she would. Hoping to never return home. Longing to stay in this forest of sandstone people forever.

She imagined letting the water rise higher still until it swallowed her whole and the ocean flowed deep inside and she merged with the salty water and 'Genna' was no more.

Suddenly she realized that she had sunk deeper and deeper with each retreating wave. The undertow had caught her to the thighs, her legs almost cemented in quicksand,

and Genna had to struggle for her life as each wave drew her further down and threatened to engulf her. She ducked under the water to dig fast and deep into the saturated sand to extricate herself, swallowing brine, knowing she would be buried within a short time and dragged out to sea. Just as she managed to free both legs, the water rose above her head.

Gasping and choking, she did not know how to swim but fought her way to the craggy rock face, pulling herself up the cliff by shaky arms, quaking as terror roiled through her young body. Finally, she reached the top and stood trembling, staring at the spires. Why had she gone down there? Had they enchanted her?—she didn't believe that. But, she could have drowned! Maybe she should have!

Whatever lesson she had learned that day was reinforced when she arrived home wet and sandy. Her mother had broken the hairbrush—the worst and final beating of her life—and that night forty years ago, on her sixteenth birthday, she ran away.

"Did you pull me in that day?" she asked the spires now, their silent, dark forms outlined against a grey sky deserted by the sun. "Did you want me to join you? Were you trying to save me? Why are you here?"

Like a response, the wind gusted hard, whipping her hair into her face, snapping her coat around her legs, rattling the dried leaves on nearby trees. The waves were building and she sensed a storm rushing towards shore. She turned to leave.

Suddenly a sound stopped her.

Genna . . .

Had someone called her name? She turned in all directions, finally her eyes settling on the motionless pillars. That sound was joined by other sounds, confusing her. At first two, then more, then many, a syncopated harmony, a high-pitched choir of discordant voices—no, not voices! The sounds reminded her of steam whistles, haunting, otherworldly, but each one a different tone, shrilling, shrieking out her name.

It must be the wind, crying through the pores of the obelisks, she told herself. But the mournful wailing built to a scream. Genna covered her ears; that didn't help. Soon her own cries joined the others: "Stop. Please, stop! I just want this to stop!"

Genna . . . the otherworld whistled, *Genna* . . .

Tears gushed from her eyes. "Is this my fate?" she cried. "To be with you? To be like you? To die here? Is this what you all want from me, what you've always wanted from me?"

The mournful whistling grew louder, sending chills racing up her spine, and her body quaked in terror. These haunting ghosts demanded she capitulate to a preordained destiny. Her feet felt planted in the soil of the dead and she could only sob and scream in horror as a new spire rose above the cliff before her eyes, one that seemed all too familiar.

She had been obligated by a promise made to her mother, who insisted on it over and over for sixteen years. *Return. To the cemetery. To the graves. To visit my grave.* And Genna had kept her promise. That was all. She could go now. But her mother was shrewd and knew she would wait, watching the water, mesmerized as always by the spires, because her mother had found her here so often. But couldn't she go now? Leave this cursed place forever, and . . .

An immense wave crashed over the cliff, pulling back hard, dragging her towards the sea. She grabbed a post of the fencing and felt it give. She let go of the metal, staggering to keep her footing, and watched the iron fly into the air then plunge down to stab the sea. The second the waves and wind lulled enough, she turned and ran, even as another enormous wave crested and tried to snag her from behind.

But as she had reached the gate: *Genna . . .* The monster monoliths whistled. A mournful sound from beyond the grave. *Genna . . .* Her name, her mother's voice, her father's voice. All the generations calling as one.

She raced back along the path through darkness and ferocious wind, the sea crashing in her wake. She fled into the town, past her fearful childhood home, to the safety of her car. Even inside, with the windows closed, she heard the morbid whistles beckoning her to a grave.

Shivering, hair and clothing dripping, her trembling hands so wet they slid along the steering wheel, she started the engine and drove out of Innsmouth quickly, gasping at a pace synchronized with the thudding of her heart, the eerie sounds now imbedded in her brain.

Drive carefully! she warned herself. The storm was chasing her. The whistling acted like an audio vortex, trying to suck her back. If she had an accident, if she died here . . . they would bury her with her ancestors!

She risked a glance in the rearview. Through the gathering fog of night, the spires stood like rigid mourners at a funeral, patiently waiting for the corpse. She could still hear their wailing, the cries of loss, and suspected she always would.

Genna floored the gas pedal then watched until the black mist had devoured all trace of Innsmouth and its mourning people.

Sympathy for the Devil

They treated him like a monster. Everybody did. And he didn't deserve that. He didn't do anything. Nothing at all. He wasn't responsible, it was the others. He was the victim here. A *real* victim. All this nasty business because of that stupid woman . . . It was soooo wrong.

The nurse arrived and went about the work of nursing, *sans* comfort. This one was young and fairly pretty, with brown hair and eyes, though a little plump for his tastes, but she did the things the other nurses had been doing over the last week since he's regained consciousness into this living hell. She took his temperature, blood pressure, heart rate, all that from the automatic readings so that she didn't need to have any physical or verbal contact with him. Yeah, he was a pariah.

"I'd like my pillow fluffed," he said, not because he needed it fluffed—that wouldn't matter. He just wanted to see how she would react.

Her head jerked up as if she hadn't heard a sound in ages. Without even a glance in his direction, she moved to the side of the bed, pulled the pillow out from behind his head, made a great show of pounding it into a new shape, then, carefully, pushed him forward with latex-gloved fingertips against his shoulder as if touching him might infect her in some way. He couldn't even feel it through the fabric of the hospital gown, but that, too, didn't matter. In fact, it was a plus.

Once the pillow was in what she deemed to be the right

position, she moved his shoulder back. Without a word, she hurried from the room as if he might have the audacity to ask for something else and she had to get out of earshot fast.

"Bitch!" he muttered to her back. "Every last one of you!"

Now that he was back from the dead, so to speak, he was bored. Seriously bored. It was just a question of when they'd let him out of here. He could use a drink. And a cigarette. Neither one was possible in this place. The only thing that cut the boredom was the pain. He didn't think he'd ever been in such physical pain, not even as a kid when his asshole step-father beat the crap out of him for killing the neighbor's cat. That was nothing compared to this.

At least he had a morphine drip and he could self-regulate. With both arms and legs in casts, he had to gum the clear plastic tube hanging beside his head. He did that now, only to find that nothing came through the tube. He glanced up; the morphine release syringe hanging on a tripod next to the bed was empty and the stupid nurse hadn't changed it. But she wouldn't, would she? None of them would. They were punishing him. They were like sheep, sentimental slobs, soap opera addicts so pathetic they'd hang on every word of a sobbing woman. But he was the victim here. The *real* victim. Look at his body, broken, bandaged from head to toe! And now, craning his neck had caused pain to slice through his shoulder and back as if a hot rod had been plunged into his muscles. Yeah, and look how they treated him!

"Hey," he yelled. "Hey! Somebody get in here and turn on the damned TV, will ya?" But nobody came, of course. Why should they? They blamed him for the accident. Well, damn them to hell, it wasn't his fault!

When he woke up, the TV was on. His eyes focused on the small screen. A soap. Right. It would be. The bed next to his was empty, had been, as if they didn't want anybody too near him. Fine with him. They could all go to hell!

"Mr. Hammersmith."

His head jerked around. "Who the hell are you?"

The old woman smiled one of those beatific smiles that only the old and nearly toothless can manage. "I'm Mrs. Shade."

"Shade? Like window shade? Or are you shady?"

She laughed, one of those sweet-old-lady laughs that most people seem to love. Harmless old broad. Annoying old hag.

"What are you doing here?" he demanded.

"Oh, I'm just a volunteer, Mr. Hammersmith. I visit people in hospitals and other institutions, those who have no one else visiting them. People alone often feel a bit hopeless. I just want to help."

"Yeah, well, I don't need or want your help, but you could change the channel." He nodded towards the TV where some boy was crying and a man was holding him. Yeah, right. Real life. Bullshit!

As Mrs. Shade switched channels, stopping at a game show, she said, "Mr. Hammersmith, I have the feeling that you're lonely."

"So much for your feelings, lady. Not lonely. Not at all."

That damned smile again.

"Well, I came by when I discovered you'd not had any visitors or even next of kin who might phone or visit. Everyone should have someone who cares what happens to them."

"Ha! Like you care! You're just an old bat with nothing to do before you die." He could have laughed but he wasn't in the mood. "Look, lady——"

"Mrs. Shade."

"I'm just recovering from a bad accident and want some peace and quiet so if you don't mind——"

"Oh, I wouldn't deprive you of that. Certainly not. I'm sure you're in a great deal of pain and——"

At her words, a fierce and fiery snake shot through his spine. His mouth opened involuntarily and a cry slipped out. He rode the pain for the long moments it slithered through his spinal cord, desperately biting on the clear tube for morphine that was not there. "Damn those bitches!" he yelled when he could articulate it. "Fill the goddam morphine!"

"Here," Mrs. Shade said, "let me help you. I'll get the nurse."

She trundled out of the room at a snail's pace, which he saw through his fog of agony, returning with the young nurse. While he writhed internally, they chatted like he wasn't even there, and certainly not in extreme and relentless pain.

"And I worked as a nurse before I retired, but that was a dozen years ago. My, this apparatus is much more complicated than in my day. Do you have children, Laura?"

The nurse named Laura smiled and said, "Yes, a toddler. He's twenty months and getting to be a handful."

"Oh, that's the age! I remember my daughter at two . . ."

And on and on they nattered while the nurse took her damned time changing the morphine syringe in the machine. Finally, she was done and the two douchbags walked out the door together. But what did he care. He gummed the tube and saw a couple of drops run down into the needle stuck into the vein just above the cast covering his left arm. The drug kicked in at last and he exhaled wearily.

The old woman poked her head back in the door and said, "Is there anything else you need before I go?" That stupid smile again. "I'd be happy to bring you books and magazines."

He didn't even bother answering her, just closed his eyes and bit down on the tube again.

"You'll have to appear in court," the lawyer was saying, staring only at the papers and not at his client.

"Why? I didn't do anything. It wasn't *my* fault."

The lawyer, whose name he thought was Lawson or Lawrence or something like that had been appointed by the court to represent him. Not that an innocent man needed representation but, as they say, the man who represents himself has a fool for a client, and he was no fool!

The lawyer paused for a moment, barely glanced at him, then said, "Be that as it may, the law is the law, and you'll need to appear in court for sentencing. Your history of impaired driving won't help but I expect your injuries could work in your favor when I ask for a continuance. If that's denied, perhaps the judge will take your estimated recovery time of a year into account when sentencing."

"Right!" He snorted. Damned lawyers and judges. What did they know about pain? It was all so wrong.

"As I've told you, the law stipulates two to five years for involuntary manslaughter but the judge has discretion to reduce that, depending on circumstances. If we're lucky, you might serve six months, or no time at all in jail, especially if you can show remorse."

"Why should I be remorseful? I didn't do anything wrong."

The lawyer looked at him blankly, licked his lips, and then went back to his papers.

"All right, Mr. Hammersmith, let me go over with you again how——"

"We've already been over everything. Twice. That's enough. Get out!"

The lawyer had a look on his face that said he wasn't used to being talked to this way. He sighed, gathered the papers atop his briefcase and slid them inside, screwed the cap on his expensive-looking pen, then stood. "We'll continue another time, when you're feeling up to it." He made his way out of the room as one of the orderlies came in with a food tray.

"Supper time!" the cheerful young punk said. Arms full of tattoos, skin studded with metal, hair in one of those modified-for-work old-school Mohawks, the color bile green.

"Jesus! How come they let people like you work here?"

The punky kid's smile turned to a scowl. "Maybe because I'm caring and sympathetic, even to sociopaths?"

"Go to hell!"

"If I do, Mr. Hammersmith, I'm sure I'll meet you there! You probably run the place."

At that, another pain shot through his spine. But, dammit, he wouldn't show this kid he was suffering.

The punky orderly placed the tray on the table and moved the table so it stretched across the bed, then uncovered today's lousy meal. He glanced at Hammersmith. "Too bad you're in pain. But, at least you're alive."

The pain left him speechless so that he couldn't respond.

"I'll be back in a few minutes to feed you," the orderly said, turned and walked out.

Once the pain subsided, he caught his breath. The nauseating smell of mushy, micro-waved food filled his nostrils and cut off any sense of hunger. Just as well. By the time the punk orderly returned to feed him, the food would be cold, just like it was every meal, every day. They were all blaming him.

This was so wrong.

"Mr. Hammersmith. May I call you Evan?"

"Who in hell are you?"

"I'm Reverend Francis, of St. Margaret's, the church down the street. Mrs. Shade mentioned you and as I was already in the hospital visiting a palliative-care patient, I thought I'd just drop by to see if you needed anything."

Great. Now they were hell-bent on saving his soul. Like he had one! "I don't need anything, Reverend. Wasted your time coming here."

The minister smiled and took a seat. "It's never a waste of time to minister to one of God's children."

"I'm not a child and I don't believe in God. Or the devil, unless that's me, which everybody seems to think I am. What I do believe is that earth is a hellhole."

The minister smiled patiently. "Well, whether or not we believe in God, He believes in us."

"I don't think your God believes in me, unless he's a sadist. I'm the victim and I'm being treated like a criminal."

Reverend Francis had clearly heard statements like this before. "God forgives all, even if the people around you don't, or can't."

"What's to forgive? I was in an accident. My body is broken. Maybe your God can forgive everybody who's blaming me for something I didn't do, but I can't."

The minister paused. "You were driving that night."

"Of course I was! And?"

He paused. "I believe you'd been drinking."

"I'd had a glass of wine. Is that a sin? I guess it is in your books."

"Your alcohol level was far over the limit."

"What is this, the Inquisition? I had a bit to drink, like people do. What's the harm?"

"The harm is that a woman was seriously injured, with brain damage, and her——"

"Look, that stupid woman crossed against the light. That's not my fault."

"Mr. Hammersmith, under God's law, when one takes responsibility for his actions——"

Pain zapped through his arms and legs, starting at the

base of his spine and shooting out as if he'd been electrocuted. He barely had time to yell, "Get out. Now! Get the hell out of here!"

He was only vaguely aware of the minister leaving. Pain racked him, zigzagging, alternating sharp then dull, the signals hopping along his nerves to the endings then back again until he could hardly breathe.

It seemed to go on for minutes but he knew it could only be seconds. The pain had been growing worse each day since he'd regained consciousness. All the broken bones from when he flew through the windshield and into the air then slammed against the tree. Everything broken. He'd lost consciousness quickly and that saved him from knowing about it then, but now . . . Now that he was *recovering*, the pain just kept intensifying and all the morphine in the world wasn't enough.

He chewed on the drug drip anyway, trying to get enough into his system to allow him to lose consciousness, even though the tube wouldn't give more than his daily dose, which he'd reached. His throbbing head fell back against the pillow. Everybody was wrong. *He* was the victim, not the stupid woman who walked in front of his car. Not her stupid kid, and at least the kid died fast and didn't suffer, not like he was suffering.

If that religious guy was right and there was a God, he saw no sign of him. And besides, if there was a God, any God, then people should know that and stop blaming him for something that wasn't his fault anyway. It was *her* fault, not his! What a sick world!

"I've brought you a few magazines, Mr. Hammersmith." It was that old whore again, hobbling into the room, placing the magazines on the bed beside him.

"Yeah, well, you may have noticed I can't really hold a

magazine to read it, can I?"

She looked a little befuddled, as only old people can. "Oh. Well, perhaps I can read to you."

He sighed heavily. "Look, lady——"

"Mrs. Shade."

"Right. Look, thanks for the magazines but no thanks. Just go. Don't come back."

Instead of leaving, Mrs. Shade took the seat by the bed. She reached out a hand and touched his torso, about heart level, where his rib bones were broken. Through the sheet and the hospital gown he felt heat flowing into him.

"What in hell are you doing?"

"Just making contact, Mr. Hammersmith. Heart contact. I wanted to feel your heart beating."

"Take your hand off me, lady, or I'll call for the nurse."

She smiled that sickly-sweet smile again and said, "Oh, Mr. Hammersmith, I'm not sure she would come, are you? I really do understand that they've been treating you like a monster. But then, they blame you for the accident."

She removed her hand and suddenly a ferocious pain stabbed him in the chest. The fierceness of such a knife-edged attack left him breathless, unable to speak, to scream, to do anything but lie as if comatose while the nerves in his chest exploded. Maybe he was having a heart attack!

Sweat broke out from every pore and his muscles trembled. He was going to die. This time, the pain would kill him, he just knew it! Well, damn it! Bring it on! He didn't mind dying. He minded physical pain!

Through the ceaseless agony, he heard the old woman say, as if reading his mind, "No, Mr. Hammersmith, you won't die. Not yet. You're still relatively young, with much life left in you. This too will pass."

He'd gotten through enough of the physical torment that he could snarl at her, "Pass? You think this will pass? It's not passing, it's getting worse!"

"Things get worse before they get better."

"Take your fucking platitudes and get out!" he gasped, his vision still blurred, but the pain seemed to be easing a little. He caught a few deeper breaths, and felt the trembling subside. As his vision cleared, his body shivered from cold; his hospital gown was soaked.

"Let me help you, Mr. Hammersmith. That's what I'm here for."

"I-don't-need-help," he growled between teeth still clenched again the attack.

"Don't you? It seems to me that you do. I know Reverend Francis was here yesterday. And I know you sent him away too. But really, this isn't getting better, its worse, isn't it? And most of your pain is because you don't accept your part in what happened."

How dare she! The old bat was hitting him when he was down. That's the only reason he could think of that he was even listening to all this BS.

"You know, lady, it's a good thing I'm trapped in this hospital bed. If I wasn't, I'd have kicked you out on your ass by now!"

"Mr. Hammersmith. Everyone is guilty of something. It's just a question of fessing up. It's that simple. Admit your part in things and life becomes easier. For you, for those around you. It's a simple exchange, really. You give something, you get something."

He wanted to yell at her, no, *scream* at her. He longed to be able to leap up out of this bed and throttle the old bag!

"Really, Mr. Hammersmith. I don't think you have anything to lose by admitting that you drove drunk, that it wasn't your first accident while drunk, and that you are directly responsible for killing a child and severely and permanently injuring her mother. You have a lifetime of cruel, callous and unconscious acts, monstrous acts that have resulted in pain and suffering for others. It's a fact, all of it. Admitting it can only easy your pain. Give yourself a break, Mr. Hammersmith. Do that, and others may give *you* a break."

He longed to be free of these casts so he could throw her out the window! But suddenly the bad sensations returned, without warning, turning his body electric again with high-voltage sparks of blinding, searing pain. He could barely stay conscious. His body shuddered, close to convulsing, staggering though immobility, unable to stand the onslaught.

"Admit your responsibility, Mr. Hammersmith, and the universe will open new doors. One thing in exchange for another. That's a rule of life; the old goes out, the new comes in, and change occurs. You'll be a different person, I guarantee it."

It was as if one of those doors opened inside him, one clear and pain free. He saw a door in his mind, one with a transparent window that beckoned: *Enter here.* Something was on the other side of that door, something better than this and he thought: *What the hell, what the hell, what the hell . . . ! I've got nothing to lose. Anything's worth a try! At the very least, if I tell her what she wants to hear, she'll go away!*

"Okay, okay, I did it! All right? Did you get what you want?"

"Did what?"

"I was drunk. I had drinks."

"And?"

"And what?"

"The woman."

"Okay, I didn't see her. Or the kid. Maybe I saw the kid, I don't know. Okay? Is that it? Is that what everybody wants to hear? Satisfied?"

"I think the universe is satisfied, Mr. Hammersmith."

He gummed the morphine tube and found it empty again. "Shit!" he yelled.

Mrs. Shade looked at the self-regulator, then stood. "I think the tube might just be twisted. I'll fix it for you."

While she worked on the machine, she said, "You know, admitting guilt is really only the first step."

He bit the tube. Nothing. Then, finally, a couple of drops.

"There is still the question of reparations."

Before he could respond, in a split second, as if a magnet had sucked the iron from his body, the pain disappeared. He blinked in disbelief. "What the . . . ?" His body hadn't felt this light, this pain free . . . ever! He began a laugh that plunged to his gut and soon turned uncontrollable.

"I don't believe it! It's gone! The pain is gone!"

He turned to the old woman. "It's gone!" he said again, feeling his face stretch into a smile of astonishment. "You were right! All I had to do was take responsibility for what I did and now I'm free."

She reached over and patted his chest with that warm-like-fire hand. "I'm happy the physical pain has dimmed, Mr. Hammersmith. I think things have resolved the way they should and you're now where you deserve to be. Admitting guilt. Free of physical pain. Now there's only restitution."

He laughed, almost crying in relief. For the first time since he'd regained consciousness, his body felt alive, real, pain free. He just might recover after all.

Mrs. Shade hobbled to the door and he called out after her, "Hey, lady, good tip."

With one backward glance, she grinned. "My pleasure. And I'm so pleased to have met you, Evan Hammersmith. Oh, and by the way, have you guessed my name?"

He felt confused. "Guessed your name? I don't get it. Your name is Shade, right? Mrs. Shade?"

"In one sense it is, Mr. Hammersmith? My daughter is Gheena Lewis, *nee* Shade, and Suzy Lewis was my grand-daughter."

His breath caught. The woman and kid he'd hit!

He thought for a moment, quickly rearranging the letters of her name in his mind but he didn't get far with that before he noticed her grin looked oddly toothy. He realized that what he was seeing didn't really resemble teeth. These were sharp and pointed, a mouthful of daggers. Not just that, but her face was morphing before his eyes. The sweet-old-lady look altered as if the lines imbedded in her skin ran together, drawing a roadmap of deeper lines gouged in flesh that took on the quality of parched, abandoned earth. The whites of her eyes disappeared completely until the entire eye was red with a black glow behind. The dry, crinkly skin of her arms, her hands, her legs, all of it distorted until she became something *other*. Gruesome, grotesque. Terrifying!

His throat constricted and his skin turned clammy. His heart fluttered madly in fear. He registered surprise: fear, an emotion. One he did not remember ever feeling. Like lava racing down a mountainside, a range of scalding emotions washed over him in fiery waves, as intense as the physical pain that had vanished. Guilt, grief, remorse, horror, self-loathing... Responsibility. A lifetime of responsibility for a lifetime of irresponsible actions, for all the pain and sadness he had caused others and the negativity he had spewed into the world.

"What's happening to me?" he cried.

And in an instant, as the demon before him laughed and glanced at the morphine drip, he knew. She had changed the syringe.

"What did you drug me with? What?"

"You wouldn't know the chemical name, but it's a drug used for torture. Oh, and the effects? They seem to be permanent. Fitting, don't you agree?"

Whatever invaded his bloodstream forced back the physical pain and filled him with emotional pain of equal weight. Killing emotions that sliced him to ribbons and left his mind reeling. Emotions he did not know he was capable of and with which he had no knowledge of how to cope.

"It's that deal-with-the-devil thing, Evan Hammersmith. And the devil got her due!"

The demon laughed, the sound grating, rubbing his anorexic soul raw.

The thing that retreated, eyes gleaming like the fires of hell, whispered in a voice that caused shivers up his spine and sent his mind reeling in terror, "Welcome to *my* Hades, Evan Hammersmith. Prepare yourself for a long and well-deserved stay!"

Evan sensed his reason slipping down a bottomless well. Finally, he saw clearly why everyone else despised him because now he hated himself. Self-loathing left him hopeless. Despicable, inhuman, unlovable, he longed for release from this unbearable dark weight of who he was. If he could move, he would jump out the window to his death, but he could not move, and would not be able to for a long long time. Time that stretched before him: hours, days, weeks, months, years of scalding emotions, agony, and no relief in sight.

He screamed for help, but no one came. There would be no sympathy for this particular devil.

The Oldies

In one way, it seemed inevitable. That, of course, flies in the face of the idea that we mortals can control our destiny. I used to be one of those who believed that. Now, I don't know what to believe.

What I am sure of is that I'm chilled to the bone with the underpinnings of a reality that I've skirted past all my life, a reality of not what we *know* but of one we *sense*, lying like a magma just beneath the crust, pushing to erupt. We feel the heat of it, praying to whichever deities fit our upbringing, or the metaphors we have developed an interest in over a lifetime. Praying for intervention. And yet, when I think of doing that, after all I've seen, after all I've been through, such an approach seems as insane to me as the madness of the reality hovering just below our consciousness. And that's what leaves me utterly terrified, unable to sleep at night, tormented in the daylight. Questioning everything that I formerly believed, or maybe more, *hoped* existed in the universe.

How did I get to this state? Like almost everything in life, one step taken leads to the next. A choice, the road taken or *The Road Not Taken*, as Robert Frost wrote so poignantly. And then suddenly, there you are. Here I am. But it began innocently enough . . .

I had been friends with Kinsey for several years. We met in a therapy group sharing Sophie, the therapist—an eclectic sort of counsellor—with eleven others. Our group of thirteen *analysands* as Carl Jung would have called us—and indeed, Sophie had been sculpted by Jung's ideas, though she herself was not a Jungian therapist but had trained as a Freudian who had settled to that number and the group remained cohesive.

We met regularly, twice a month on a Wednesday night, and initially hung out in Sophie's waiting room—with her blessing—after the two-hour sessions. That gave us a chance to get to know one another in a more relaxed and 'normal' way, though perhaps not as deeply as through the psychic flotsam and jetsam that drifted to the fore during the actual group.

The range of all-female personalities: twenties to fifty-something; married, single, separated, divorce; heterosexual and lesbian and one transiting gender to male. The unemployed to the professional. Some were more introverted and tended to retreat to their homes after our bi-monthly sessions. Others had children or other dependents to look after, so they too were gone. The leftovers, without much of a social life, included Kinsey—a twenty eight year old artistic woman in a relationship with the extremely patient and nurturing Henry; Cheryl—our twenty-two year old unemployed self-described *token*-in-the-making transsexual; Gwen—our jokingly self-described *token black spinster* and head of nursing at a large hospital and also, at fifty-five, the oldest of the group; and myself, Cat, perennially single, good office job, no life, on her way to becoming Cat the Crazy-*Cat*-Lady pushing forty. The four of us frequently met for dinner between therapy weeks, or at our favorite pub, *The Eleusinian Mysteries*. The on-tap beer list wasn't extensive, but we got a kick out of the name.

We were all neurotic, not psychotic, at least not then, and I remember distinctly the evening we met at the pub when the problems started, when Kinsey announced, "Last night

I tried to kill myself."

Gwen gasped. Cheryl gripped the edge of the table. I froze, stunned but not surprised. We all knew Kinsey as vacillating between mouse and monster, meek and angry. And highly dramatic. While we reacted in our individual ways, Kinsey's lips twisted into a smile, but her eyes turned glassy, haunted. That odd combination alone sent a chill up my spine.

Finally, Gwen asked, "What happened?"

"I got into the tub with Henry's razor, unscrewed it, took out the blade, and cut one of my wrists." She pulled up the left sleeve of her sweater and we saw a large gauze- and medical-tape bandage wound around the wrist.

"That's not the best way," Cheryl blurted out, "going across the vein, I mean."

We all understood Cheryl's obsession with doing everything *the right way*. Not one of us hadn't thought of or attempted suicide in our life. All four of us had been cutters in our teens, trying to cope with too many feelings and no outlet—we had that in common—and we all understood the best way to ensure death was to cut along the vein, not across it. But, of course, that was irrelevant.

When I found my voice I asked, "What precipitated this?"

"Nothing," Kinsey said.

"Something must have happened. Did you and Henry fight?"

"No. Not at all. We fucked after dinner, then he went to sleep for a while in his chair and woke up to watch a basketball game. I had a bubble bath—lavender. The idea just came to me in the tub, out of the blue."

"I thought you'd given that up," Gwen said a bit sternly, "indulging in suicidal thoughts." None of us wanted to be judgmental but we also didn't want to enable Kinsey's destructive impulses.

"I did. It just happened."

"You'll have to tell Sophie."

Our next session opened with Kinsey repeating to the entire group what she'd told us. A calm and clear-eyed woman, our leader Sophie had a weight issue but, other than that, she seemed to be a paragon of sanity and a boulder we all leaned against for grounding, especially with such a dire revelation.

After Kinsey finished her tale, many exhibited or stated reactions that ranged from shock to fear to fury, some of the above accompanied by tears. Finally, Sophie said, "Kinsey, let's go back to that night. Tell us again what happened."

Kinsey repeated the sequence of events she'd related at the pub and just after making love with Henry, Sophie stopped her. "Did you enjoy the sexual experience?"

"Yeah. Sure. I guess."

"Did you have an orgasm," Beth, one of the angrier women in the group wanted to know.

"I guess. I think."

Sophie held up a hand to let us all know she was headed somewhere and to butt out. "Talk about what you felt."

Kinsey took a minute. "Nothing. I felt nothing."

"Look into that nothingness. What do you see in there?"

"Just a black hole. Where there could be something, but there isn't."

"A black hole has energy. It pulls things in and absorbs them."

"Yeah, I guess."

"Did you feel absorbed?"

"Maybe."

"Let yourself be absorbed by that darkness. Don't be afraid; we're all here with you."

Kinsey closed her eyes. The room fell silent. Suddenly her body jerked.

"What are you experiencing, Kinsey. Tell me what's happening."

More silence. More jerking. And then Kinsey's voice, but somehow younger. "I'm in a room. It's empty. Dark as midnight, cold like winter, no life. There's no one here."

"How do you feel?"

"I don't feel anything."

"Are you afraid?"

"No. I'm relieved. There's no one here. Just me."

"Do you feel safe?"

Kinsey paused. "No."

"Why?"

"Because . . . I know they're out there. And coming."

"Who? Who is out there?"

"The Oldies."

"Are these people you know?"

"They're not people."

That sent a wave of trepidation through the room, one that set my body to trembling.

Sophie spent the rest of our session and even went overtime trying to get Kinsey in touch with what had precipitated the suicide attempt. Every aspect Kinsey mentioned of the evening she attempted to off herself was gone over and over as she was pressed to delve into whatever feelings were there. Sophie, no doubt, hoped to get to the core of what drove Kinsey to such thoughts, and action. And while at first Sophie tried to investigate *The Oldies*, Kinsey couldn't or wouldn't go near that. She couldn't define or describe or identify in any way who or what they were, only that she had encountered them before, when she was young, and she just sensed that they were coming.

Sophie left it alone and extracted a promise from Kinsey that she would phone if she felt this way again or became depressed, or angry. In other words, suicidal.

It was a frustrating night for everyone, unsettling to be sure, and after our session only Kinsey and I remained in the waiting room. She looked pale to me, but then she had been put though the mill.

"Are you okay?" I asked.

"Not really."

"Do you want to go for a coffee or something?"

"No. I just want to sit here for a bit."

We sat in silence for what felt to me to be a long time. I didn't know what to do or say so I said and did nothing. Finally, I looked at my watch; it was after 11 p.m. I had to get up early for an important meeting, but I didn't want to just ditch Kinsey.

Suddenly she turned her head and looked at me, the brown of her irises in the dimmer light of this room melding with the black pupils. Her face and lips were very pale now, accentuating her dark brown hair, brows and eyes, and there was something eerily ghost-like about her. "I'm not going to win against them," she said. "No one can."

"Who?" I asked, but I knew the answer.

"*The Oldies.* None of us can win. You can't win."

I don't remember what I said, but I remember trying to be reassuring and comforting, letting her know that whatever inner demons she was encountering would *not* win, I was there to help her, the group was there to support her, Sophie was good, she would find a way, Henry loved her. All the things you say to someone who is falling apart before your eyes while at the same time you feel spooked.

That night my dreams were nightmares, littered with dark places, crammed with rooms like black holes, pervaded by a sense of someone or something unpleasant that was just on the other side of the walls. I woke three separate times in a sweat, heart racing, breathing erratic, hands trembling, upsetting my cats. Needless to say, the following day was hell for me.

I was exhausted the next night but still I phoned Kinsey and she said she was all right—I suggested we go to the pub and she agreed to that. I called Gwen and Cheryl. Gwen was fine with meeting for drinks but Cheryl said she couldn't do it. It was too freaky for her. She couldn't expose herself to that much negativity.

So, three of us met at *The Eleusinian Mysteries*. Kinsey seemed like her usual self, and that was a great relief for Gwen and me. We didn't talk much about what Kinsey had done—and she claimed it was just a fluke, it wouldn't happen again. Mostly we drank and laughed and chatted about nothing, trying to overwhelm her darkness with the light of life. Gwen and I thought it worked.

Our next group was taken up with all the feelings brought about by Kinsey's suicide attempt. Everyone verbalized their reaction. Kinsey said virtually nothing—what could she say? *Sorry?* That made no sense. And in therapy, the point is to deal with your *own* feelings and not the actions of the person that 'caused' those feelings in you.

Cheryl was still upset and didn't want to hang out after, but Gwen and I were ready and willing. Kinsey, though, decided to go home early. "I haven't been sleeping well. I'm tired. I think I'm catching a cold and just want to go to bed," she said.

Gwen and I stayed.

"Do you think she'll try it again?" Gwen asked.

"I hope not. She seems more stable, just, like she said, tired."

"What do you think about what she brought up last time."

I paused. "You mean about *The Oldies?*"

"Yes."

"I don't know what to think. Sophie kind of hinted it was

a psychic break that wouldn't happen again."

"Did she say it wouldn't happen again? I didn't hear that."

"No. Just me hoping."

"I hope too," Gwen said. "All this reminds me too much of my childhood."

"What do you mean?"

"You know I was born in Haiti, right?"

"Yeah. You left when you were a kid?"

"Yes. I was seven. But I remember very clearly a ceremony I saw. I went with my mother, just before she died of the cholera she'd contracted after a hurricane. It was a *Vodou* ceremony. They killed a chicken and smeared blood on sick people like my mother to heal them. The *Bokor*—a female priest who serves both the light and dark forces—spoke in tongues and looked like she was out of her mind. Quite a few people looked that way. And Kinsey looked that way to me."

"Do you think *Vodou* is involved?"

"I don't know. I only know what I saw as a kid and what I saw two weeks ago, and it looked pretty much the same to me."

"Gee, Gwen, as far as I know, Kinsey's never had anything to do with Vodou, or any other religion. She's an avowed Atheist."

"I know," Gwen said. "What I mean is, the haunted look on her face, tonight, last session . . . that's how the *Bokor* looked. And . . ."

"And what?"

"The *Bokor* talked about serving the spirits, *The Old Ones*."

That left me unnerved and led to another sleepless night.

During the next two weeks, I tried to gather our small group again at *The Eleusinian Mysteries*. Kinsey said she had a cold. Cheryl still needed to keep her distance. Gwen was busy with work and her granddaughter had just had her tonsils out so grandma felt the need to spend evenings with her.

I had plenty to keep me busy during the day, and in the evenings two non-therapy friends to connect with for the ballet and a touring musical about to close. I even had a date with Frank, a computer techie from work that I'd been seeing off and on for six months or so. He wasn't the love of my life—though I doubted I'd ever find my soul mate—but it was a nice break, dinner at *Chez Ennio*, the latest superhero movie, sex. At least I slept that night.

Kinsey didn't show up for our next therapy session. I wondered if her cold had gotten worse. 'Psychotics never get sick' I'd read in some article or book once, so I found that reassuring, even if it might not be true.

Sophie started the group with an announcement. "I need to let all of you know that Kinsey is in the hospital."

The moment of silence was palpable.

Sophie didn't pause. "She tried to commit suicide again two nights ago, this time a more serious attempt."

The next two hours were spent with group members crying or shouting or curling into near fetal balls, the gamut of emotions.

Just before we concluded, Sophie told us, "Henry said visits would be welcome," and she gave us the name of the hospital.

Cheryl was a mess and rushed out after the session. Everyone else looked upset and fled for home. Gwen and I walked to the subway together without speaking. We took the train in the same direction and as we sat in the crowded subway car, she said softly, "I have a very bad feeling about this."

"Me too."

"I'll try to see her during my lunch break tomorrow, since the hospital isn't too far from my hospital."

"I'll go after work," I promised. "I guess she'll be on medication."

"Probably anti-psychotics."

This was grim news. No one in our group was on serious meds. It wasn't that Sophie was opposed to it, and she could prescribe, but it just happened that the group members' issues were not severe enough beyond short-term usage of tranquilizers or sleeping pills. At least not until recently.

Work was insane. The project I'd been involved with for weeks at the ad agency needed quite a bit of tweaking, and that took up the entire day. Frank wanted to meet on Friday, but I reminded him that a co-worker's bridal shower was that night, so I was only free on the weekend, but he would be out of town then. We arranged a tentative date for the following week. To tell the truth, I felt unenthusiastic. I was upset about Kinsey and dreaded the thought of seeing her later that night.

I walked slowly through the antiseptic-smelling corridors of the large hospital. The walls had been painted puce at one point when that color was fashionable for institutions, but now the hue looked tired and depressing.

When I reached the right floor and corridor, I saw Henry standing at the nurses' station, talking with one of the nurses. As I approached, he turned in my direction. He looked awful.

We had only met twice, briefly, at Sophie's holiday gatherings where friends and spouses were invited, but still we hugged. "How are you?" I asked.

"Holding it together."

I nodded. "And Kinsey?"

"They've got her on strong drugs. She's a bit of a zombie,

so be prepared for that."

He took a break and went to the cafeteria so we could visit privately.

I entered the room to find her paler than I'd ever seen her. She was propped up in the bed, wearing the requisite pastel flowery hospital smock, her eyes more glazed than ever.

I walked to the side of the bed and took her hand and she stared blankly at me. "Hi," I said. "How are you doing?"

"Fine." Her hand was limp and cool. I could see that she had bandages around both wrists and up her arms. "I took Cheryl's advice," she said. "*The Oldies* told me to."

I inhaled sharply. The cuts had to have been up the veins; if she'd hit an artery, she'd be dead. And, again, talk of *The Oldies*. I didn't know what to say. Despite that, and knowing she was drugged, I asked, "How did *The Oldies* tell you to do that?"

"In a whisper," she said.

The room felt chilly to me but, obsessively, I persevered. "What did they say?"

"Do it. Just do it. *Now.*"

That sounded like an old ad slogan to me and I wondered if it was something she'd heard on TV, so I asked that.

"No. The TV was off. I was in the kitchen, making dinner. Henry was on his way home from work. The dog had been fed. I was paring potatoes and carrots for a stew."

"So . . . you . . . heard them?"

"Yes. And this time I saw them too."

I felt my hand holding hers twitch and the room seemed colder. "What do they look like?"

"I don't know."

"But you saw them."

"Shapes. Big shapes. Bigger than the universe."

I was out of my depth with this, and wasn't sure how to

go further and just then a nurse came in to take readings of blood pressure, oxygen saturation, etc. and saved me.

I waited out in the corridor with Henry. "Did she mention *The Oldies* to you?"

"Yes," he said, his face and voice tense with worry.

"What do you make of it?"

"The doctor here said she had a psychotic break. They have her on anti-depressants."

"What do they say about her prognosis?"

"They feel it's good. These meds have been prescribed a lot and have a record of working on this kind of illness with few side effects."

I wasn't so sure. And why I had doubts I didn't know at that time.

We went back into the room together and I stayed another uncomfortable twenty minutes, avoiding the subject of *The Oldies*. I did, however, mention it to Sophie privately, who told me she'd been to see Kinsey several times and had the same information.

To say I felt unnerved would be an understatement. But life goes on, and while I did visit Kinsey twice more before she was released from the hospital, we didn't talk about anything contentious again.

Henry, a teacher, took a leave of absence from his job to stay with her 24/7. I hoped for the best but feared the worst.

Four months later, Kinsey rejoined the group. She had been doing individual counselling with Sophie during that time, which must have helped her, because she looked better. Her face had regained some color, and while she seemed a little stilted, there was something of the old Kinsey in the way her full lips smiled and how she spoke.

Sophie cautioned us that although there were many emotions that needed to be expressed, we couldn't do it all at once, and Kinsey couldn't take a barrage, so we would need to move slowly over the next few sessions.

Kinsey looked to be heavily medicated and yet functional, to a degree. It had been, she said, her decision to return to the group.

"I wanted to explain to you all why what happened happened," she said, her voice flat, her eyes flat, her skin suddenly paling to an unhealthy pallor, and I began to worry.

"The voices have been with me since childhood. I heard them as far back as I can remember. They weren't voices I knew, and they talked like adults, chatting to each another, mostly ignoring me. Sometimes they told me things I should do and I did them and that got me into trouble. When I was young, I talked to them, even when they ignored me, but my parents tried to put a stop to that, telling me they were imaginary friends and I needed to find real friends and would in school.

"I've heard them all my life. They seem to be everywhere and speak whenever they want to. I can be alone or with people, when I'm painting, at a concert, reading a book, at a ball game with Henry. Having sex. They still tell me what to do and I don't feel I can go against them. I've tried; it doesn't work out well."

She held up her wrists showing us the angry red wounds.

"They don't just tell me what to do, they also like to tell me things, as if they're teachers educating me. Like about the universe and how empty it is. Not empty of stars and planets but empty of meaning. They say there's no god, just them, and that we humans are nothing at all, specks of dust. Less even, meaningless, and they only come to us for their amusement, but we're not always amusing and we're not that interesting."

She stopped and everyone seemed to hold their breath

until Sophie asked, "What do they mean by their *amusement?*"

"I don't know, but I've felt that for them it's like us watching a movie or TV show or even sitting in a cafe watching people. It's something to do."

"Yet they manipulate you."

"I guess. They say it's for my good, what they suggest."

"Do you think it's for your good?"

"I don't know. Maybe. They tell me that life is pain and there's no point in continuing. That's what some of them say. Others say I should keep going, because you never know what's around the corner."

She paused and I know many of us wanted to question her further, but at this point, getting the whole story out was probably the best way to go, or so it seemed then.

"One thing I do know—they're not happy that I talk about them."

"Why?" Sophie asked.

"Because." She paused again, looked down, and when she looked up her face was different. Her eyes looked like glass eyes and held a kind of inhuman, demonic glint. Blood had rushed to her pale face turning it almost crimson, and her full lips had formed a rictus exposing her teeth. "They say that some of you hear them, but you try to block them. Anyway, you can't block them. They're too powerful. They control everything, everywhere, every one of you. And they can prove it even though they don't have to prove anything, but they want to, just for fun."

"What does that mean, *just for fun?*" Sophie asked.

Kinsey looked down again and reached into her shoulder bag.

When she looked up, she not only *looked* different, but now seemed like a completely different person, one none of us knew.

She pulled from her bag a large knife. Everyone seated around her jumped to their feet, and most fled to the door or the corners or anywhere to get away from her.

"Put down the knife!" Sophie, standing, said firmly. "Kinsey, put it on the floor."

"I'm not Kinsey," she said, her voice lower, and now she was talking with an accent. A German accent. Her face seemed more angular. "*Ich bin Hitler! Sieg Heil* to me!" She thrust out her arm holding the knife.

Sophie approached her cautiously.

Then Kinsey's voice changed again, and her skin seemed to darken. She spoke with the accent of an African speaking English, the tone jovial . . . at first. "You know me, Idi Amin Dada, your friend. And I, I know you very well, all of you, my girls. Come!" Suddenly the tone hardened. "I put your heads in my freezer!"

Then a Spaniard speaking an accented, staccato English. "You are all guilty! Confess! Confess to Tomás de Torquemada. If you are guilty, you die slowly and painfully; if you are innocent you die the same!"

Amidst the horror of a succession of continuing voice changes of the madmen of history, I don't know where I gathered the courage, but I came up behind Kinsey on her right. At the same time, Gwen came from her other side. Together with Sophie, the three of us were encasing Kinsey, whose back was close to the wall. But we were wary. She spun from side to side waving the knife at each of us, slashing out, all the while Sophie trying to talk her down.

"We're on your side, Kinsey. We'll help you. We're your friends. You need to put down the knife and we can help you."

Kinsey became still as a statue and this, to me, was one of the most alarming moments because she looked like a standing corpse. Instinctively, Gwen and I both inched

closer to within just a couple of feet from her. Our eyes met
in understanding and we were about to grab her arms. Instantly, she snapped her head left, then right, over and over,
the inhuman deranged look stopping us in our tracks. And
then her psycho eyes fixed on Sophie.

Suddenly, a macabre, otherworld sound reminiscent of
hollow laughter erupted from her. The voices mixed together, joined by others, as if dozens were speaking and
laughing at once, none of them Kinsey, and it was terrifying.
"Kill her!" "Kill them!" "Kill them all, now!" "Drop the knife,
Kinsey. Everyone loves you." (The last voice imitating Sophie's!)

Then the unthinkable happened. Kinsey still pointed the
knife blade at Sophie. In a fraction of a second, she turned
the blade inward and stabbed it into her heart!

Screams filled the room. Pandemonium ensued. I remember holding Kinsey. Blood all over her. Over me. On the
floor. Shrieks coming from Kinsey. Gwen keeping the knife
in place to prevent further damage. Sophie talking to Kinsey. Everyone dialing 911 on their cell phones.

I was told the ambulance arrived within minutes, but at
the time it seemed to take forever. Many of the group fled.
Gwen and I stayed until they took Kinsey away. And all the
while Kinsey sobbed, "They didn't want me to tell. They said
not to. I did anyway. I shouldn't have. They don't want to be
known except on their terms."

While the situation was sharp in my mind for many days
afterward, over time the details have blurred. I know that
Sophie went to the hospital with Kinsey. Gwen and I were
rattled and we talked and talked but nothing made sense at
all. It took me more than a week to visit Kinsey because I
was in a state of deep shock.

I entered the room in the hospital's psych ward in trepidation. Kinsey had never looked so clear-eyed, so sane. And

yet what she said by way of a greeting was anything but. "They came to me, finally. I could see and feel and hear them, so it's all good now. I think it's easier now, if you know what I mean."

"I don't," I said, my nurturing instinct pushing to take control but my decisive brain, which I'd spent days with analyzing the situation and my role in it, was determined to be the leader this once and keep my emotions from ruling me.

"I'm free now," she said, a beatific smile lighting her pallid face.

Henry had told me that the knife missed her heart by a mere two inches, but punctured a lung. He was at his wits end, he said. He didn't know what to do. Sophie recommended that Kinsey be placed in a facility for a while where they watched suicidal patients 24/7. Henry wasn't sure about that. He didn't like the idea of her "being locked in a back ward somewhere". He felt Kinsey belonged with him, in his care rather than in a cold institution. By his side, he said, was the best way to go. He was taking a long leave of absence and preparing for them to go into the woods together where things were always better, camping for an extended time, connecting with nature, like they used to, where Kinsey felt safe and sane.

I wasn't convinced of his plan, but then I saw no alternative. Yet one thing I knew for certain—I had been traumatized. Something in me cracked at the core as I watched her taken over by *The Oldies* and stab herself with a six-inch carving knife. The horror of it was too much. I'd reached my limit and I knew that to be in touch with her, with this, again, would destroy me. I'd come to tell her that.

"Kinsey, I need to say something."

She nodded.

"I think of you as a friend, and I've tried to be a friend. But I can't handle this. This is too dreadful. It's beyond what

I can cope with. I love you as my friend, but I can't be around you."

She didn't look upset or sorry. She just said. *"The Oldies* told me you would say that. Goodbye Cat." And she smiled.

Disconcerted, I mumbled, "I wish you the best," turned and headed for the door. Only to hear a sound follow me out that sent waves of horror zipping into every pore of my body aiming for my soul. Multiple voices. Deep. Laughing. The same macabre laughter as when she had stabbed herself, aiming to sever her heart.

The inhumanity of the hollowness was so alien I had the sense that no person had ever encountered it before. I certainly hadn't. My instinct was to flee, or to turn, to see *The Oldies* however they manifested with my own eyes. I fought the latter instinct, hard. Instead, I hurried out the door, carrying the reverberation with me clouded by the scent, because a foul and offensive odor clotted the air. Beyond decay. The combination of everything brought a word to my mind and I whispered it: "Entropy."

Life has not been easy for me since. The group continued but with immediate dropouts—our numbers fell to seven— then more left as we tried to unpack *ad nauseam* what we felt about Kinsey, about what happened. There was no rationalizing the sheer, all-pervasive horror we had experienced collectively and individually.

As we struggled to make sense of it, many ideas and concepts were discussed. Gwen brought up Vodou. Someone with a Catholic background elaborated on demon possession. Schizophrenia was covered. None of it felt like a comprehensive answer. The closest to resolution I came was when Sophie talked about Carl Jung's thoughts on the dark side of the archetypal energy we call *God*.

Then, one night, Sophie told the four remaining in the

group that when Kinsey was released from hospital the week before into Henry's care, he began preparing for their extended camping trip in the woods. Last Friday evening, the night before they were to leave, she disappeared. The police searched everywhere. Officers were waiting in the outer room to question us, which they did, but we had no new information or even guesses to offer as to her whereabouts. After the group, Gwen and I headed to *The Eleusinian Mysteries*, but Kinsey was not there. She seemed to have vanished.

The funny thing is, somehow I already knew all this. I'd gotten home from work exhausted that Friday and after I fed Lucy and Allan, my two Siamese cats, I opted for a nap before dinner. I dreamed of the smell, and the hollow, alien sound. The nightmare woke me at 8:30 P.M. Sophie told us that Henry noticed Kinsey missing around 9 P.M.

Shortly after that night, our therapy group disbanded. Despite the monstrous events that had occurred, I was sad to see the end. I felt that I had gleaned some good things over the three years. Gwen and I have kept up a friendship of sorts, although we only see each other once every six or eight weeks or so, and we never meet at *The Eleusinian Mysteries*.

As the seasons switched from spring to summer to fall to winter, then back to spring, my life took a few more unexpected twists and turns. Frank proposed and I said no. A month later, he married someone else. I quit my job for one with slightly lower pay but much less stress. And I acquired another cat, a black rescue already named Darkness who resisted a name change and terrorized Lucy and Allan, and found myself well on the road to Crazy-*Cat*-Lady-hood.

I felt I had reached some stability. Not happiness, but then that was a goal I'd given up long ago. That I'd reached a plateau would be a more realistic statement. Life was not bad and not good. I had some financial security and was still young enough to date again, should I ever have the opportunity, or the inclination. Besides my cats I had other interests like theater and a pottery class, my two non-therapy friends for the occasional dinners and shows, yet I felt emotionally flatlined, but I didn't mind that. Kinsey popped up in my thoughts now and again, the unpleasant feelings blanketed by time.

Until the Saturday when Gwen phoned. "Have you seen the news today?"

I said I hadn't.

"Go look. Then phone me back."

In trepidation, I went to the Internet and found what I knew she was referring to. The bones of a woman had been discovered in the woods north of the city. Experts believed she had been there since the previous spring, animals and insects having at the corpse, plus the elements of a year's worth of heat and cold decomposing the flesh until only bone remained. Dental records provided an identity—it was Kinsey.

I sat back shocked. This was not expected but, at the same time, not unexpected. There'd been no word of her, no sign since the night she'd left almost a year ago, her purse and credit cards abandoned on her dresser, wearing brown slacks, a white blouse, and leather jacket and boots, the remnants of which were found with the bones.

What I hadn't anticipated was what would happen next.

Within a week of the news, Sophie sent an email that she was retiring and moving to Europe, country undisclosed, offering no contact information. The last time I saw Gwen was a week after her phone call. We met at *The Eleusinian Mysteries* for 'old time's sake' to 'have a drink to Kinsey.' And while we talked about her, about the news, about the past, about the anguish we both felt, Gwen and I did not discuss the future. I could see from her haunted eyes what she likely saw in mine—*The Oldies*.

Since the night I read about Kinsey's remains, *The Oldies* have been coming to me in odoriferous nightmares, voices masked, words vague, the many hollow sounds unintelligible, layered one upon another, alien cries and laughter and emotions I cannot understand or identify, that scrape at my soul like a thousand knife points. *The Oldies* whisper to me, night and day, whenever they feel like it, playing games with my mind, pulling me this way, that way, and in ways I could never have envisioned until I am dizzy and drunk and scared by the confusion. When I can think clearly, they seem like demonic, all-powerful children. They remind me of a clowder of cats, frustrated and bored when the prey succumbs. Kinsey's demise has left them with no one to play with; I am the new toy.

I try to ignore them. I tell them to shut up. I weep in despair, beg them to leave me in peace, scream out my rage at being violated. My music and TV volume are cranked to the point where my neighbors bang on the walls. Nothing works. I can still hear them, smell them, sense them, everywhere.

I don't know how this will end, how it *can* end. I resist the urge to do myself in, but I feel I'm being worn down. My destiny is no longer in my hands and my fate seems inevitable. Because Kinsey did, I know I will see them and when I do, it will mean my annihilation. That's the game they play. It's all a game, and one I can't win. No one can win. You can't win either!

The Visitor

Ian jolted awake. *Where am I?* Bleary-eyed, he turned his head and saw the red digits on the clock radio—1:00 A.M. Something was *very* wrong, he felt it!

Heart thudding, his flesh unpleasantly slick beneath the covers, sinuses totally clogged up from the flu or virus or whatever the hell had attacked him the minute he'd arrived on the Caribbean island of Grenada, he lay still, struggling to calm his thundering heartbeat, fighting for control of his breathing, desperate to keep from having an asthma attack!

Little light came through the nearly-closed slats of the Venetian blinds, but it was enough to see that both the room and closet doors were closed, the bathroom door was ajar the way he's left it, that tiny room empty, but he couldn't see the shower, which was behind the door.

Darting glances told him no one was in the room with him—how could there be? The outer door—the only door—was locked. The screened windows were barred from opening more than four inches. He took a deep, calming breath, hearing the rattle of mucus in his chest, blindly reaching for his inhaler on the night table and then remembered he'd left it in the bathroom, and felt disheartened.

The thought had been good. Get away from the stress of work, of life, but really the emotional turmoil of a relationship that had run its course and was now certifiably dead, or so Rob had decreed.

Ian had found a brochure in the coffee room at work listing this island he'd never even thought of visiting, one so far south it could have belonged to Venezuela when France, and then Britain took possession of the land until 1974, the year Grenada gained independence, or so the brochure said.

This spontaneous get-away had Ian on a tight budget—as usual, especially since he'd been abandoned two months ago in the expensive apartment—why had he agreed to put the lease in just *his* name? Well, because Rob said it made sense and he'd keep the utilities in *his* name, so they'd be equally responsible. Except that the utilities in Rob's name and been cancelled and Ian had to set up an account and fork over a deposit when the lights and stove stopped working.

This *resort*, not really a resort, more a little motel with a pool, was located at the southern end of the island, two miles from the airport, far from the famous *Grand Anse* beach where the well-to-do stayed. Ian's unfashionable digs were a lot cheaper, if a little distressed. But the Caribbean Ocean was close enough, a five-minute walk, although he'd only been there yesterday around 9:00 A.M., just after he'd arrived, hoping the sea air and the gentle waves would soothe his hurt soul. But the waves were violent, the sky black with the coming storm, and the wind nearly blew him into the salty water.

He decided on a nap after the early flight, hung the *Do Not Disturb* sign on the outer doorknob, thinking *I'm disturbed enough!*, and finally crawled into bed, asleep in seconds. He didn't wake until around ten last night, only to discover that he'd come down with the plague. *Perfect!* What could be better, alone, abandoned, sick, in a strange land and his cell phone didn't seem to be working down here.

He'd never been anywhere by himself before, certainly not outside the U.S., so that alone made him nervous. But he didn't know what else to do. Two months without Rob in his life after three years with him *in* his life allowed a heaviness to descended over Ian like a lead weight pushing against his heart. His job was affected to the point where his boss suggested he take time off, or think about leaving voluntarily, permanently. He couldn't really afford either, since he was now stuck with the apartment rental *and* utilities, but Bonnie and her husband Lou—friends since high school—had insisted he needed to get away, even just for this very short but cheap weekend. They contributed a third of the cost, "An early birthday present," Lou said. "Fly out Friday night, arrive Saturday morning, fly home Sunday night," Bonnie added. That seemed doable to Ian. It would have been the right thing to do if he hadn't gotten so sick. Maybe he could spend the weekend sleeping . . .

The white blades of the ceiling fan directly above the bed caught his attention. They sliced the air like knives, a soft whir. Other than that, the utter lack of sound was so unlike life in Cambridge that he found the silence disconcerting.

And then he heard another noise. A small noise. In the room!

"Okay, calm down!" he ordered himself for the twentieth time, this time aloud, wheezing. "You've had a dream, that's all," more like a nightmare, one he couldn't remember and likely didn't want to remember. He was in a strange bed, in a strange country where it was too hot, away from the familiar—which was the whole point of coming here. "Of course you're nervous," he reassured himself, sucking in air to a too-familiar rattle in his chest. "Who wouldn't be?"

Rob wouldn't be, that's who! Nothing upset Rob. He was a rock, logical, stoic, stable emotionally, all the things Ian was not. And Ian had relied on that rock to hold him up, at least he used to; now he had to rely on himself and that was hard. Almost impossible. He'd always been *high strung* his mom declared, and despite all the effort in the world, controlling his emotions was a twenty-four seven fight, a battle he'd continually lost over the last couple of months.

He was a wreck, and he knew it. His world had collapsed and he couldn't cope. And now he was in a strange place, alone, and it just made everything worse! *One more day*, he thought, then *I get on a plane for home*, and immediately he began worrying about terrorism on the flight, or insane passengers, or delayed or cancelled flights, mechanical failure that would drop the plane into the ocean where he would drown and be consumed by fish! His wheezing increased.

In the darkness he reached for his almost useless cell phone on the bedside table and checked the time: 1:11 A.M. *Right!* he thought, *the spooky time*, and he then reached for a tissue from the box to try to unclog his sinuses and in pulling one up, knocked the box to the floor.

Finally, with a weary sigh, he pushed the thin blanket and top sheet off his hot, sweaty body, instantly feeling cooler. It was hellishly humid here, even in the middle of the night. He wondered how anything could stand living this far south—and this was winter!

The air from the fan was a relief at first but Ian realized that it probably wasn't a great idea to get too cool, so he pulled the covers up to his neck.

He was just thinking about picking up the box of Kleenex and going to the bathroom to pee and get his inhaler when he heard the sound again. A kind of soft crackle, as if paper was being crumpled.

Immediately his heart began thumping. With a groan, he swung his feet to the floor and turned on the bedside lamp, squeezing his eyes shut at the blast of incandescent light. He held his woozy head in his hands for a second until the room stopped spinning and he acquired a fragment of control over the wheezing. Then, under the safety of the illumination, Ian scanned the room. Nothing and silence, just the fan. The sound was probably from outside the window directly across from the bed. He felt like an idiot. Stupid. A wuss. The way he always felt about himself, but now, add to it that physically he felt like shit.

He heaved a bigger sigh of exhaustion, the rattle from his bronchial tubes depressing, and sat up, swinging his feet to the floor. He had to pee. And retrieve the inhaler. He bent and picked up the Kleenex box and placed it back on the table.

Maybe that's why he'd woken up. He was sick. He needed to be upright, as always when he got bronchitis or flu or a cold or whatever caused his bronchial tubes to swell so he couldn't easily inhale or exhale air.

The room, now infused with light, looked the same as when he'd gone to bed. The red eye of the TV, the other red eye of the smoke detector in the ceiling, the multi-red eyes and slashes of the clock radio, the alarm set by the last resident of this room, apparently. His suitcase sat on the floor where he'd left it after a quick unpack of a cooler outfit before flight fatigue overwhelmed him and he'd decided to wait and stash the case in the closet in the morning. His passport and the keys to his apartment sat on the narrow counter that held a microwave and some plane snacks they had passed out instead of a meal—a mini bag of veggie chips, a packet of roasted cashews, and a second Coke he'd gotten gratis from the flight attendant who felt sorry for his no-doubt mournful face, but then he decided not to drink it.

Ian shoved himself off the bed with a groan and stood on wobbly legs. Now he felt chilled. He stumbled to the bathroom as quickly as he could, peed, flushed, didn't bother with soap just a quick water rinse of his fingers, grabbed the inhaler off the windowsill—he was shaking now from the chills and had to get back to bed!

He switched off the bathroom light then, on second thought, switched it back on as a memory from childhood of demons in the darkness flitting through his consciousness.

If he closed the door partially there would be just a line of light along the bedroom floor but not enough to disturb his sleep, at least he hoped that would be so.

He grabbed the Coke on his way back to bed then perched on the edge of the bed, pulling the top sheet and thin blanket he'd found in the closet earlier around his shoulders like a feeble old man. He'd better use the inhaler first before he had the Coke, or should he have a drink before the Ventolin raced through his system and got his hands shaking and his heart racing at 120 bpm. *Keep hydrated*, came to mind, something his mom would have said. And then he remembered Ventolin dried out his mouth and throat too, so he pulled the tab on the can and took a good swallow. The harsh, sweet cola tasted great, so he guessed he needed it, and he downed half the liquid before he placed the can on the bedside table.

Silence. Chills. Wheezing. He needed sleep. He picked up the inhaler.

Suddenly that sound again, paper softly crackling. This time he identified it—over by the window, under the window, between the trash can and his suitcase, nothing more than two-feet from anything else in this small room. *Maybe it's a rat!* he thought, suddenly terrified. He should go look. But he was afraid. He glanced around the room quickly, searching for a weapon, seeing nothing. Then he remembered a broom in the closet of this efficiency room.

He placed the inhaler on the table as quietly as he could, stood naked on trembling legs, paused—silence—then tiptoed the five steps to the closet and took hold of the narrow door's knob. *What if there's someone, or someTHING in there?*

'You're so paranoid,' Rob had always accused. 'You're afraid of your shadow.' He heard Rob's voice as if he were in this room and had just said that!

But Rob had been right. Ian *was* afraid of just about everything. Anything could go wrong at any time. But with Rob's encouragement, he had started to let go of some of his automatic fears, and then—boom! Rob had gotten tired of him. No, Rob had met someone else! Ian's biggest fear, one Rob had always reassured him would never happen. Until he *stopped* reassuring him and Ian sensed something was very wrong, and . . .

'Get a grip!' Rob's voice again, a snarl this time, and Ian knew he was hallucinating. Chilly now, he trembled, his exhale a suffocating gurgle of not getting enough air in or out that assured him he would never really get a grip.

He turned the knob and pulled open the narrow door. The bedside light showed him that inside was only an iron and ironing board, an empty shelf where the blanket had been, hangers on the pole, one holding a bag of liquid he had been told would absorb moisture so his cloths wouldn't get mildewy. Finally, a broom and dustpan.

Ian quickly snatched up the broom, unsnapped the dustpan from the handle and placed it on the shelf, then suddenly turned by instinct towards the small trash can near his suitcase under the window near the foot of the bed. And was astonished to watch an enormous, round bug—it had to be two or three inches across—crawl over the rim of the can, down the side to the floor, move forward half a foot and stop. It seemed to be looking at him as if sensing danger.

He didn't know what to do. He didn't kill bugs, even though he thought them disgusting, and this huge one particularly so. He caught them and put them outdoors in nature—an action Rob had always mocked him for. A quick look at the microwave shelf told him there was nothing he could use to catch this giant, shelled insect that was now exercising its wings as if it could fly! Maybe he could sweep it towards the door and out. Yes, that's what he would do!

He leaned back from the closet to the room door that led to the courtyard and twisted a little so he could open the lock. In that moment, he heard a distinct "No!"

His head snapped back. The insect was running in circles. And that scared Ian so much his wheezing intensified.

On impulse, he stepped towards the bug—it really was big!—and tried to catch it with the broom and thought he had. He began one quick and deliberate sweep towards the open door but when he swept out the door, nothing went onto the outside landing.

"What . . . ?" And then he saw the bug racing up the broom handle. He let out a small shriek as he threw the broom away from him.

Before the broom hit the wall, the bug unfurled its wings and leapt off the handle in midair—yes, it could fly! It landed in pretty much the same spot as where it had started—between the trash can and Ian's suitcase—then raced under the bed.

Now it was Ian's turn to yell "No!"

He grabbed up the broom, bent and began sweeping under the bed, the bristles sideways so that they would pull everything out into the open. Nothing, just dust bunnies. Panicked, he did it again and again.

As he was about to give up, wondering how he would be able to sleep with this giant flying cockroach under his bed, the broom brought out the bug!

Ian tried to sweep it towards the door again but it disentangled itself from the bristles and before Ian could react, it ran the other way, moving faster than any insect he'd ever encountered, behind the trash can, up the wall of the little counter towards the snacks and the microwave, then right-angled and disappeared into a crack where the counter met the wall.

"No!" Ian said again, not quite so loud, not wanting to

wake other guests who would see him in this naked, *hysterical* state, as Rob would have defined it. And Ian did feel like a madman.

He closed the room door, picked up the broom and leaned it against the wall in preparation for further battle, then, feeling like the loser in a tournament, sat on the bed, shoulders slumped, head in hands, body no longer chilly but now blazing, so hot that sweat seemed to gush from his pores. Everything looked strange, as if this place was not a physical environment but a dream world, and he wondered if he was dreaming, or awake. Or dead. The wheezing from his chest assured him he was neither dead nor dreaming. He was suffocating, gasping for air like a fish pulled from the water.

Ian picked up the salbutamol inhaler, did a test squirt to make sure the medication would come out, then exhaled a big, ragged breath, then with the opening of the inhaler surrounded by his lips, pressed the little canister down into the top end of the inhaler's elbow-shaped pipe to take in the medicine, sucking relief deep into his lungs. He repeated this twice more.

He felt the Ventolin doing its job, relaxing the small muscles in the walls of the airways, allowing breath to flow in and out without the wheeze. Within minutes the clenched muscles relaxed completely, the obstructed bronchial tubes had unblocked, and he could breathe almost like a normal person again.

The enormous swell of heat subsided and with it the intense sweating. But now he was getting cold again so he wrapped himself in the top sheet and blanket and took a sip of Coke, which no longer tasted wondrous.

Ian was used to the side effects of the asthma drug but had never gotten comfortable with the jackhammer heart, the quaking body, the headache that was not always present but when it was, it was a doozie. There was a list of other possible symptoms, some of which he suffered occasionally. But one symptom was psychosis! But he wasn't psychotic, or at least he *hoped* he wasn't.

He'd already started to tremble uncontrollably and was aware of his heart beating so fast and hard that it set his body to quivering even more. This was much worse than usual after using the inhaler, and worse than the flu symptoms, but maybe they'd mixed together. As always, he'd just have to wait it out. Hadn't his mother always said—

"Keep calm. This will pass."

Ian jolted. Rob's voice again! *Who said that?* He looked around the room. Now that he could breathe, he not only felt more confidence, but he had the liberty of once again thinking about the giant bug and what to do.

As if on cue, the bug tentatively exited the crack in the wall in three stages of movement, then stopped and perched on the edge of the counter, antennae waving frantically in the air. It didn't make a move towards or away from Ian.

"Don't overreact!" it said, and Ian knew that the bug had said this, in Rob's voice, and this was quickly followed by, "You're not losing your mind. I'm your spirit animal."

Unable to stop himself, Ian blurted out, "You're not a bear or a wolf or a raven or an eagle, how can you be my spirit animal? You're just a bug! A cockroach!"

"Palmetto."

"What? What are you talking about?"

"I'm a Palmetto. You know, from the Palm trees."

Ian's heart still raced but the speed-like drug made his head much clearer, and he felt brave, for once. "Why are you talking in Rob's voice?"

"I'm not. You're hearing his voice, like a translation from Palmetto to English."

Ian grabbed his head just as the headache began to form.

"This is crazy. *I'm* crazy! I'm losing my mind!"

"You're just emotional. You've got to calm down."

"Don't tell me to calm down!" and Ian's hand shook as he reached for the can of Coke, so jittery he knocked it over, the remaining contents spilling onto the tile floor. "Now look what you made me do!"

"Ian, take it easy. You really are stressing yourself for nothing. It's just liquid. It will dry. If you want, I'll come over there and drink some of it if that will help."

Ian grabbed his head as it began to throb in earnest. "Go away. Please! Just . . . away. I'm having an aneurysm!"

"Such a drama queen! You're *not* having an aneurysm. It's just a headache from the meds." Something Rob would have said. And still in his voice.

"I'm losing my mind! I'm about to have a stroke! I'm talking to a roach!"

"Palmetto."

"God, stop!"

The creature was silent and Ian spent the next few minutes trying to control his quaking body, pounding heart, breathing deeply and slowing, struggling to relax his brain muscles so the headache would dim. And had enough success that he could contemplate mopping up the Coke.

Finally, he stood, walked to the bathroom, scowling at the bug *en route*, who seemed to be following his movements if the shifting antennae were any indication. Washcloth in hand, he went back to the cola spill and mopped up as much as he could, having to rinse out the washcloth and repeat. Finally, he left the washcloth in the bathroom sink, came back to the bed and trembling, re-wrapped himself in the shroud of sheet and blanket to counteract the flu chills that had now replaced the asthma-treatment symptoms.

"Ian, I think you should sleep now. You'll feel better with some sleep." Rob's voice again. But Ian also decided that sleep was the best solution to everything, the flu, the asthma, the Ventolin, the hallucination of a giant insect talking in Rob's voice. All of it would dim and hopefully disappear with sleep. He lay back and closed his eyes, leaving the night table light on. He wanted to cry. Instead, he nodded off.

Ian awoke to the sound of laughter and chatter. The sounds came from outside his window and he remembered the pool was in that direction so it must be guests using the pool. He heard one man say something about dinner on a ship docked on the east side of the island and two women with British accents agreeing that it sounded like a brilliant idea.

He sat up, feeling dizzy, and still sick. Once his head cleared a little, he got his feet to the floor and noticed it was sticky. Right, the spilled Coke. The broom stood against the wall. It all came rushing back to him.

"Talking to a bug. I'm really losing it now."

He'd missed breakfast and if the clock was right, lunch too, but he wasn't hungry. He staggered to the microwave and retrieved the bag of veggie chips, pulled it open and ate a few, then a few more while listening to the laughter and chatter outside from normal vacationers, then noticed the bag was empty but for crumbs, so he tossed it into the trashcan, opened the foil packet of smoked almonds and ate a few, and then put the packet back on the counter. He walked to the bathroom, peed, washed his hands, took a long drink from the tap and filled a glass with water for the night table, hoping foreign germs did not worsen his condition, and turned off the bathroom light.

Despite all the sleep, and the sheets damp and unpleasant from sweating for hours, he climbed back into bed. The rattle in his chest was mild and he decided to not use the inhaler again until absolutely necessary. He'd try to sleep more and hope that the rest would cure him. *It might not help but it can't hurt,* his mom always said. He switched off the night table light and sighed as his head hit the pillow.

When he woke again it was dark out. The lights in the room and the bathroom were off, and he only heard the soft whir above him, so it took a moment to remember where he was.

"Are you awake yet?" came Rob's voice, and Ian tensed and held his breath. He sat up abruptly, waited out the ensuing vertigo now accompanied by nausea, then with a shaky hand reached over and switched on the lamp.

There it was, where it had been the night before, between the trash can and his suitcase, seemingly staring at him, antennae waving in his direction. Ian didn't even bother with formally being shocked or repulsed by the creature or the voice. He just got right to it. "What do you want?"

"You need help."

That made Ian laugh bitterly. "You want to help me, huh? By driving me crazy? I'm a sick man, or hadn't you noticed?"

"I noticed. It will pass."

"Oh, you're a doctor too, not just a roach."

"Palmetto. And no, I'm not a doctor, but my species has existed since the beginning of time and we're aware of many things, like vibrations. You're not at death's door."

"Thanks for the encouraging words." Ian knew he sounded petulant and didn't care. If he was psychotic, so be it. There were drugs for that and he'd get some when he got home ... when ... tonight! Yes! Relief flooded him. He checked the clock—four hours until the flight. He'd be out of here soon.

"So, why are you talking to me? What's this about, Mr.

Palmetto?"

"You can leave off the *Mr.* I'm female."

Ian raised an eyebrow. "Too much information."

"Not enough, really."

"So why? What do you want?"

"You need an intervention."

Ian snorted.

"Ian, I know you're suffering. But I can help. I carry the wisdom of the ages. Of the universe."

"Right. With Rob's voice."

"I told you, it's a translation issue. His voice is one you recognize and you give it authority."

"Not anymore!"

"Are you sure about that?"

Ian took a sip of water. This insect had his number. Maybe he was nuts, hearing Rob's voice, talking to this lowest of the low creatures, but hey, he was still pretty sick and had nothing much else to do before the flight, so he might as well converse with a roach. Palmetto.

"Okay, so how are you going to help me."

"I'll give you the key to unlocking your potential."

"Oh, so you're running a motivational workshop. How much?"

"You're path involves destiny. Expediting the greater good."

"What greater good?"

"Facilitating others in need. You will help the weak become strong."

"Yeah, right!"

"Don't be so cynical." Rob's voice and Rob's exact words, and Ian sighed.

"All right, what should I do to become this powerhouse of transformation?"

"Well, first of all, you need to go home and cure yourself

of this physical illness."

"Thanks, I wouldn't have thought of that."

"More cynicism! Next, you've got yourself in a mess financially. Sublet your apartment and rent a smaller and cheaper one."

Ian had, of course, thought of that but the energy required seemed beyond what he was capable of.

As if reading his mind, the Palmetto said, "You've got to do it, even if you think you don't have the energy. It will save you money and save your sanity by not going back to that place every night that evokes memories and sadness."

The Palmetto gave Ian a moment to think that over then said, "And you've got to get back into your job. This is not the time to change jobs. Stick it out. Your boss likes you or he would have fired your ass months ago."

Ian signed again. "True. I've been a slacker."

"Exactly. You have to pull yourself up. It's over with Rob, he treated you badly, but shit happens and you've got to move on. Start with those three things and you will find yourself in a much better place."

Ian felt chilly and pulled the covers around his shoulders. "You're right. I have to do all those things. I feel so alone. I just wish I had someone to help me."

"You do. You have me. I can help you recharge your life. And the best part is, when you're solid again, I can help you get revenge."

Ian didn't like the sound of this. "What do you mean?"

"You can get back at Rob and anyone else who has ever hurt you. And don't tell me you don't want to. I can see your deeper desires."

Ian was about to protest but realized that made no sense. He'd thought about revenge a lot, on Rob, and on others, so this wasn't out of nowhere. "But how?"

"Oh, there's a plan already in motion. And there will be

help refining it. Don't worry, it's all sorted out. It's what we do. We befriend the weak and helpless and they become strong and powerful beings."

"Well, I'm not sure I want to know your plan. But how can that work anyway? I go home in a few hours. And you're here."

"Oh, I'm going with you!"

"What? No! Not happening. First of all, you'd infest my apartment. Second, you couldn't survive the cold climate. Third, what do you mean by *with you?*"

"Infest your apartment? Really, Ian? One Palmetto? And my species can tolerate extremes. Besides, your place is heated, isn't it?"

"I guess, but——"

"And when I say *with you*, I mean I'll be there as your advisor and confidant, helping you make the right decisions and taking action for the betterment of all species on this planet."

Ian thought about this for a few seconds, listening to the whir of the fan in the room cut the air. He was hot now, pushing the covers off, sweating profusely. And his thoughts had become muddy again. Was Rob's voice going to be with him forever? He had enough clarity to say, "So, what are you getting out of this, Ms Palmetto?"

"Everything. I'll see new places and observe different human beings, expanding my knowledge base of your species. After all, you humans are fascinating, your strengths and weaknesses, your insecurities; we've been studying you for a very long time."

"Why study us? We're not that interesting."

"Oh, but you are! You seem hell-bent on extinction and my species has known we can help your species with that problem because we are survivors, if you'd only accept us in your world. My offer stands. Yes, or no?"

Ian's body dripped sweat. He stared at his moist palms and thought about all that was said, or tried to, but his brain wasn't functioning. He just knew one thing: he had to pack and get to that plane. When in doubt, decide nothing, that had always been his motto. Finally, he said, "Thanks for the offer, but I can do this on my own."

He looked up but the Palmetto had disappeared from its spot between the trash can and his suitcase. Maybe the hallucinating was over. "Are you there?"

Nothing. That *had* to be a good sign.

He pulled himself to his feet, lurched to the carry-on, with effort lifted it onto the bed and then opened it. A smear of brown covered his clothes that suddenly started moving, undulating, like hundreds of Palmetto bugs, and he jumped back with a cry. Ian blinked; they were gone. Just his clean jeans and t-shirt and socks so he took them out and dressed, then tossed into the suitcase everything on the night table and the opened foil packet of smoked almonds from the counter and his toiletries from the bathroom, the clothes he'd worn on the trip down, the inhaler, and then snapped the case closed. As he slipped on his runners, he grabbed his jacket from the back of the door and the room key in one hand, the carry-on in the other.

He'd get to the tiny airport early and have something to eat there, then another hit from the inhaler—less symptoms on a full stomach. He'd be home by morning. All this would be behind him. No more flu. No more Rob-the-talking-roach. *Palmetto!* And he laughed so loud at that thought that he didn't hear the foil crackling inside his suitcase.

Trogs

We don't live in that rock cave anymore. They put a stop to that, said we had been hiding, we needed to be good citizens like all the others, and there was no room for such self-ish individualism and isolationism in the modern and better world. Now we live here, in this cave-like room made of some sort of hard, colorless polymer, windowless, the only opening the door which is sealed until They want us to come out and we go, of course, because what else can we do.

They are in control, and have been for a long long time. *They* can control us in just about every way, but not my thoughts, because now I write those down in this paper book my mother gave me just before they took her away. And maybe I don't know why because I don't expect anyone to find this in the future but I hope someone will, and read it, and see how it was, at least in my lifetime.

Writing in the paper book comforts me; it's the only thing I have from my mother. *They* wouldn't let us take anything with us and I had to hide this in the big pocket of my dress. But it also relieves the boredom and loneliness, at least a little, so, I write in the book of empty pages, blank until I fill them, the book Mom found outside the cave when she went looking for firewood. She secretly passed the book to me as *They* came towards the cave opening, whispering that I had to hide it. She told me it is an antique and I should treat it well. She called it a *journal*, so I will call it that too.

171

It's a thick book, the hard covers damaged by the elements, the pages yellowed and stiff and crinkly from the weather. My mother told me to write small because it would be the only book I would ever have, so I have learned to write in very tiny letters with a pencil that I found before I was given the book—like an omen. I want the journal to last.
The End

This Day

My grandfather, when he was alive and my brother and I were very young, and before we hid in the rock cave with our mother, he told us stories that my brother believes were lies. Grandad said when he was our age *They* weren't as strong or as smart as *They* are now. We were in control and *They* were subordinates. He said that scientists and engineers kept working to make them smarter and stronger so *They* would do more for us and eventually *They* took over because everyone thought it was a good idea and would make our lives easier if we just let *Them* run things and do all the work.

I was never sure if my grandfather made some of that up. It seems to me that *They* have always been in charge, but then I have lived only sixteen years by my mother's calculations, and my brother twenty-two, so neither of us know how it was before.

After my grandfather left us, we abandoned his house. I tried to ask my mother about what it was like in the past. By then we were hiding in the cave and she was sick a lot "from the damp" she said, because the outside air was hotter than it used to be and all the stalactites and stalagmites were melting and leaving big puddles of limestone water that we used for washing and cooking. My mother said the fumes from the water made her cough, or maybe it was drinking the water even though she boiled it, but my brother said that's not possible, limestone can't harm you, and it was probably just the humidity in the caves. That's what we thought for a long time.

She did tell me that she didn't know if her father's stories were true or not. The world she grew up in was a lot like the one I grew up in before we had to hide in the cave—just about everything was taken care of and directed by *Them*. Maybe, she said, her father's childhood had been different, but he was a good storyteller and she had never been sure of the difference between the stories of his childhood and the stories she said he read in books that had been written before he was born. "At least you can read, and your brother is better at drawing than reading," she told me, "so maybe one day you two can find out for yourselves."

I didn't know how my brother or I could find out anything, since we were in the cave all the time except when we went out to forage for food to cook and tree parts to heat the water the food was cooked in. I asked my mother where are the books my grandfather read so I could read them, but she said she didn't know, maybe in the house, but we couldn't go back there.

But now we aren't living in the cave and my mother is no longer with us. My brother is always angry and restless and doesn't like to talk with me about the past before we were born or even the past after we were born. He draws on a digital screen with colored markers, angry images of beasts eating machines, then erases them and draws more. He hates the polymer room. I don't like it much myself but it's not damp like the cave, at least, and in a way it's cave-like—the only kind of world I know.
The End.

Later This Day
They bring us nutrient pills twice a day and we swallow

them obediently. It's not like the roots and grasses my mother cooked for us in the pot that was heated all day and all night because she said we had to keep the fire going. That food she called *soup* and my brother and I could eat as much as we liked because there were still a lot of roots and berries and plants and tubers that grew near the cave that she could put in the pot. The pills aren't good or bad but they are tasteless and hard to chew, so we just swallow them. We are told that the pills are good for us and give us everything we need. That may be true, or not. I don't know what's true anymore, if I ever did. I just know that the soup was good.
The End.

A Frightening Day

One of *Them* opened the door and called us by name in a voice imitating our mother's to come outside for the daily exercise while another waited to direct us.

My brother was furious. He does not like being ordered around by *Them* and he does not like *Them* using our mother's voice. He has whispered in my ear many times that he hates *Them;* he said he wants to kill every last one. This upsets me. I'm afraid because he whispers, saying that *They* can hear us, and warning me not to speak aloud what I don't want *Them* to hear. But I am more frightened by the chaos in his voice.

I know he blames *Them* for the death of our mother. I have tried to remind him that she was sick, very sick, but he refuses to listen. I know he knows this in his heart, but his brain won't accept it. I do not know if this really is the truth but I try to accept it because it's the easiest way to live. And because I have little choice.

How does it help to blame *Them?* I have asked my brother, but he just gets angry with me and rants so I don't bother asking anymore. Nothing will change his mind, I know that, and that scares me even more. I don't think that *They* can be killed but he does not believe me.

As we went outside, my brother tried to knock over the one that unlocked the door. He shoved hard, and kicked too. *It* teetered but didn't fall. I knew *It* wouldn't. *It* seems to be made of a plasticized metal that is very strong, rust-proof, and runs on self-charging batteries, continuously charged by the sun, a sun which our mother told us to avoid because it would make us sick. But it gives *Them* life.

They appear as individuals but act together as one unit, like the bees that went extinct that I once read about when I still had books, all the insects participating and focused on common, unknowable goals. We are no match for *Them*, that's clear—my mother called *Them Indestructible*.

In our mother's voice, *It* told my brother to stop acting childish. That only made him angrier. He tried again to topple the one that opened the door, but the other one interceded, injecting something into him with a needle that appeared out of the end of its 'arm', and I screamed, "Let him alone!" These are the exact words my mother shouted when *They* came for us in the cave and my brother fought *Them* then too.

After *They* first brought us here, I was alone in this room for days and nights, frightened, but eventually my brother joined me, calmer, but not happier. He did not win then and he will not win now.

The two snagged his arms as he collapsed and then dragged him away while he mumbled and cursed *Them*, his words slurring, but I heard him repeating a word over and over like a chant, or a curse: *Trogs . . .*

I stood alone outside the doorway trembling. None of *Them* were around and I could have run away, but I couldn't leave my brother so I went back inside and wrote all this in my journal.

I cannot bear the thought of something happening to him. What would I do then?
The End.

Any Other Day

My brother has been gone for a long time—I've had the pills eight times—and I'm worried about him. I am so worried I asked the one who brought the last pills where he was but *It* did not answer me, of course. *They* never answer, just tell us what to do. I should have tried to escape when *They* left me alone at the door. My brother would have wanted me to do that. But I have nowhere to go, and I can't leave him. I'm afraid. What will become of me without him? There's nothing I can do but wait.
The End.

This New Day

The door opened and my brother just came in but he doesn't seem like my brother. He is smiling in an artificial way and my brother has never been happy in any way, real or feigned. He says he has been re-educated and that everything is wonderful now, as it should be, and I should be happy too. And then he crawled into his bed.

Something is wrong with my brother and I have hidden my journal from him, but I don't know why. It just seemed like I should do this and our mother always said I should follow my feelings.
The End.

Another Day or More

I am writing now because my brother sleeps, and he sleeps much of the time. Since his return, he sleeps most of what must be the day and is more awake at night.

Before *They* took him, he rarely slept. He told me he could not sleep, he had to be on guard against *Them*. He doesn't seem to feel that way anymore.

I don't know what to do, but there's nothing I *can* do, just hide what I write, just in case, but I don't know what that *in case* may be. I'm not sure my writing will survive and I'm not sure anyone would believe what I write, just like the stories my grandfather told us. I only know that my brother is different now and I feel a little afraid for him but also, I'm afraid *of* him.

When my mother was alive and I was young and we had just gone to the cave, she gave me books to read that she found outside the cave until there were no more to find. One was *The Diary of Anne Frank*, about a girl who was in hiding with her family from evil people who wanted them dead. I feel sometimes like I am her. Hiding from *Them*, although they are not people. But now I am also hiding from my brother and Anne Frank didn't hide from her family. This makes me very nervous and I realize that I am starting to see my brother as I see *Them*, as not my friend, and I don't know what to do about that. There's nothing I can do.
The End.

A Different Day

My brother has taken to making things out of little sticks. Apparently, this activity is permitted and called *art*. The sticks are just a few inches long, and flat, the ends rounded so that they cannot hurt anyone. At first, he used them to build pyramids that collapsed, but he only laughed in a strange, hollow way when they did and then started again, building more pyramids.

I asked him about the sticks, why *They* brought them to him, and he said that when he was re-educated "all of us used sticks". I don't know who *all* is and asked, but he didn't answer me.

After I asked, he stopped making pyramids. Instead, he

used the sticks to create houses, boats, trees. These are things I saw pictures of in books and I guess he saw those too because they look just like the pictures, without color, since the sticks are white plastic and all the same.

I told him I thought the houses were nice and he just stared at me with the glazed eyes he has had since *They* returned him after he was re-educated. He stared as if he doesn't know me or hear me, and I turned away. I had to. His eyes frighten me.

I know I could make things too, if I wanted. There's not much to do but make something, anything, or just watch the screen built into the wall that continually shows programs that are silly, or cute stories about animals I've never seen, or young people who could be my brother and me who are *heroes* fighting ugly creatures from outer space or from the depths of the sea. I find all that boring and want to turn off the sound, since the screen can't be turned off, but my brother wants the sound on. I stuff little pieces of washroom paper into my ears and that muffles the strange, raucous laughter that comes from the unnaturally happy and brave people on the screen. I cannot think when they talk and laugh and yell and growl but the sounds do not bother my brother, who is now making different things which I can't identify.

I ask him what he is building with the sticks and he says "A home for Trogs." I'm not sure what that means but I think it has something to do with caves because I remember a word from a book about caves with those letters. I ask my brother if 'Trogs' means 'cave dwellers', but he just silently stares at me until I look away. I am afraid.
The End.

A Peculiar Day
My brother is not using the sticks anymore, now he's

drawing directly onto the walls. Every day he draws more, using black and white colored markers that *They* brought him, along with a sketch book that he doesn't use, *For artistic expression* one of *Them* said in the voice of our mother, and my brother didn't react. It was as if he'd never heard this voice before.

The drawings are large and take up a lot of space. They make me uncomfortable.

The End.

A Disturbing Day

I have watched my brother silently drawing on the walls for many days and nights now and in this rounded room he has covered all but one small area around the door, using the black and white only. I don't know what will happen when he has drawn on every inch of wall. I do not know what will happen when I fill in all the pages of my journal, and I will be writing on the last page very soon. What will we do then?

The End.

A More Disturbing Day

My brother has found my journal. He stops drawing to rapidly flip through it, from the first to the last entry, not reading, just flipping pages too quickly to read. I watch his face but there is no expression. My heart pounds hard and I am afraid.

Suddenly he comes to the final page and slams the book closed. He tosses it onto my bed and pulls out markers from a pocket of the two-pocket shirt he wears and then turns, walking slowly to the door, and begins drawing on the last small section of empty wall surrounding the door, drawing with orange and dark brown markers, the images tiny so it will take a long time to cover the area around the door frame.

I watch him for hours, a sense of dread growing. Not just

the walls, but the ceiling is also full of his artwork and the floor. We are surrounded by strange bi-colored creatures I have never seen, beings like something not of this world. Their eyes are big and dark, their heads too large, their bodies small, pale and grotesque, not only misshapen but a terrifying blend of human and animal and machine parts, and the parts of the alien monsters that always appear on the screen imbedded in the wall.

I have run out of blank sheets in my journal and have only half a page of space left, so I stop and ask my brother, "Please, tell me what you're drawing. What are these things? Tell me."

He pauses, his back to me, a magenta marker in one hand, a grey in the other, both poised above the final square foot that is not covered with bizarre images.

Instead of answering, he asks, 'Why do you keep writing?"

I can't think of a reason he will understand so I just shake my head.

He turns his head sideways. In profile, his face shows pity and then his look becomes withering. "You imagine someone will read that one day, don't you? You think something will change, don't you?"

I shake my head, but he is relentless.

He turns and storms over to me and I'm afraid he'll hurt me.

"Give it to me!" he demands, holding out a hand.

"Don't destroy it!" I beg, obeying, because what else can I do?

I place the journal in his hand and he rips it away from mine, shaking the book in the air, and now I'm really afraid that he will destroy all that I have written.

"No one will read this!" He holds the journal up in front

of his face and stares at it with his strange eyes. Then, suddenly, he tosses it at me.

I try to grab it, but the book falls to the floor and the already damaged cover falls off and pages bend further. I'm angry at him. "Maybe they will!" I shout. "You never know what will happen. You can't know."

He starts to laugh and the sound terrifies me as it fills this cave room. It is empty laugher, diabolical in its hollowness, and I have to stop him because the sound is making me feel violent and alone and hopeless. And sick.

"I'm writing for the future! For others. And I'm writing for me. Just like you're drawing for you."

He stops laughing so suddenly it is like a button pressed for the wall screen that kills sound. The look on his face is sharp grief that stabs at my heart.

"I draw because I can't stop myself. No one will see this. Even when we die, and others move in here, if others move in. It will be as if you and I never existed. You think someone will read your journal, but no one will."

"How do you know that? You can't know that!"

"I know because when they took me away, I was with many many others, the first time when we came here, and the last time when I was re-educated. Some have been here for two and three generations. Some, like me, were new. Most of them couldn't see. All the rest were going blind, either from birth, or by *Them*—they were making us blind by forcing us to stare at the sun."

I suddenly realize why he looks at me so strangely, why I fear his eyes; he is losing his sight!

A small cry comes from me and his grief turns to something cold, permanent like the glaciers I'd seen pictures of in books. Like the world our life has become.

I shake my head 'No!' and instantly my head hurts as if my skull was fractured. The pain is pointed and splitting, exploding right behind my eyes, piercing through like a honed blade to the center of my brain, and I gasp at its intensity, trembling. I lie down moaning but the pain gets worse.

My brother stares in my direction then turns away from me and begins to draw using black and blue markers in the last small square of empty space, and I now realize that with his dimming vision he had been feeling his way along the walls and ceiling and floor.

What will he do when he reaches the end, I wonder, when there is no more space to draw in. What will I do when my book has no more pages? What can we do?

"Troglobites," my brother mumbles suddenly. His arms sweep the room of his artwork. "Trogs. Endlessly adapting to the caves they live in as they go through their lives in darkness."

This room we live in is not dark, and it is not a cave, but I know what he means. Our world is dark and cave-like, his world is growing even darker, because of *Them.*

They have reduced everything to simple, and too easy, and we don't have to think or struggle or try. They don't want us to act or feel or think or struggle or try. That is inefficient. And if we do, our world darkens further.

Suddenly I do not understand why *They* have not blinded me too, and my brother, who now seems to possess a sixth sense, says, "They don't need to take your sight."

"But, why?"

"Because you're one of the last who can read."
The End.

Another Day

My brother is right, of course, and it's better this way, not fighting, just adapting.

I ask him if he will clean the images from the walls, and

my pencil has an eraser so I can erase my journal, so we can both start again, but he whispers in my ear, 'That's not the way."

He insists he needs to draw over the images he's already drawn and I should write over the words I've written, both of us creating layers. That way, *They* won't be able to know what we are doing, what we are thinking, what we are feeling. What we are trying to tell the future, if there is a future.

I watch my brother using green and blue markers to draw over what he had created, a troglodyte drawing troglobites, endlessly adapting.

I finish writing in the last small blank area and will soon begin to write in my journal on page one, scripting over my old words with new words, building word layers as he makes image layers. Even if someone in the future exists and can see and can read, they would have to study hard to decipher what we are trying to convey with our creative codes, so like multi-dimensional puzzles. But that's all right, because *They*, with all their invincible physical strength, their extreme logic and their uncanny ability to control our species, funneling us towards extinction, my brother and I are convinced that they cannot understand the peculiar illogical logic of creativity. It is our best and last and only defense against annihilation and that gives us hope.

Besides, there's nothinwegcIancadnootcahindgo . . .

Your Shadow Knows You Well

You are here by mistake. Everything is a mistake with Russell. You came because he willed it, or so it feels to you now.

This is not the type of place you enjoy, not at all. Russell, though, is enamored with the bizarre, especially the macabre, particularly with death. You made a weak attempt to warn him against entering this *museum*—the nearly-missed brass sign, the unlocked door, no curator to greet you. "It's like a horror movie," you said but, as happens when you are right, Russell ignored you.

And now you stand in a dusty, claustrophobia-inducing room, the door to the outer world slamming shut behind you, as if annihilating all life outside—if this *was* a horror movie, the door would be locked, and you are not quite sure if it is or isn't but you cannot bring yourself to check, and you know Russell will not.

Your eyes take long moments to adjust to the dimness here. Your lungs fill with what you know to be the powdery casings of insects, and the unpleasant scent of mold. Every instinct in you screams: flee! Almost every instinct. The voice in your head that orders you to please Russell dominates.

You follow him like the obedient dog you often feel yourself to be, beyond the entrance, into a chamber that somehow reminds you of the catacombs Russell took you to see in Paris, although no bones line the walls. Corridors stretch off like the legs of a spider. Each corridor leads to another room that from this distance looks exactly like the one you are standing in. Surrounding you are tall wood and glass cases, an army of upright coffins, containing . . . what? You join Russell at one case and stare at the thing inside.

This is a living human being! Or so it seems to you at first. The body is barely clothed. The face familiar because the features seem so common. For a moment, it occurs to you to break the glass and free this man who is trapped in a living death. But as you stare, you realize there is no movement. The eyes must be plastic. The hair a wig. All is so lifelike. It is as if you know this person, or knew him, and yet you are certain you have never met.

"Great stuff!" Russell exudes. He moves to the case on the left, and you follow on his heels. Inside is another body, or a wax form, a manikin of some kind, it must be, for these could not be the remains of what were once breathing human beings, people like yourself, ordinary people, caught up in a life that allows too many expectations and fulfils too few. A life which *no one gets out of alive*, as Russell is fond of joking. For you, life often feels so terrifying that you are afraid of your own shadow; getting out alive is the least of your worries.

And at that moment, you notice your shadow. Pressed across the floor. A black entity pasted into this grim environment. You contemplate the Jungian theory you studied at university when you had hopes of becoming a psychotherapist. The idea of the shadow intrigued you, opposite traits, rejected, which remain unintegrated into our being: criminal as good man, policeman as thief. How alive and sparkling such concepts seemed to you ten years ago. How alien they appear to you now, distant thoughts that you cannot bring to bear on your own life and so they have become unimportant. Your shadow is disturbingly flat. It lies limp across the floor, half way up the length of one case, as if directing you towards . . .

Russell grabs your arm and pulls you away. You are glad you did not need to see what your dark side finds so compelling.

He stops and reads aloud each plaque that identifies the person, and provides a history of his or her life—and crimes. As he reads the sixth, the seventh, the horrific stories build to demonic proportions, injecting a chill that crackles up your spine. What kind of place is this? Who has brought together all of these inhuman human monsters, this array of the worst of humanity—murderers, torturers, destroyers of lives? Russell's voice is loud in the emptiness, faintly echoing, excited, his delight obvious. Suddenly you are struck by the realization that these are not effigies at all, but are in fact preserved bodies, as if the secrets of the preservation techniques of Lenin and Perron have been rediscovered. "Somebody figured out how Lenin's been preserved," Russell says at the same moment. That you have always been in synch like this never ceases to amaze you. But there is one huge difference between you and Russell: this synchronistic connection delights him; with you, it intensifies the mind-numbing terror that eats through your soul like mold.

You watch Russell race from case to case, grabbing the wood edges, pressing his face to the glass, voice full of glee, the proverbial child in a candy store. It was his enthusiasm for life that attracted you to him in the first place. His daring contrasted with your shy, conservative nature. You know you have seen and done things because of him that, left to your own devices and permitted to dawdle in your contained and timid little world, such extraordinary experiences would have passed you by. You have come to rely heavily on him, as if your very life depends on Russell's—he holds the oxygen, each breath you take is a gift because he shares his air. Without him, you would suffocate. That he knows this and uses it to control you passes almost unnoticed now, by you, by everyone. You gave up freedom willingly at first, and after a decade together, slavery has become second nature to you.

There are many cases here, many preserved corpses denied burial. As you scan the room, you are most disturbed by the similarities. Each body seems so ordinary, like the neighbors and grocery clerks you only say "Hello" and "Lovely day" to. Like your co-workers, who you speak with out of necessity, staving off the pain of isolation. These people who pass through your life so regularly are not friends but are more than strangers. Your sister and brother, and your mother, all the family left that you have contact with, are supposed to be close, but you often feel as if you do not know them at all. Real friends have proven to be a burden, and when Russell entered your life, you gradually realized you no longer needed most of them. No one on this earth can understand the emotional chains that bind you to Russell, not even you. Your two remaining friends—Judy and Gwen—look at you with pity, and have stopped suggesting that you leave him. You see them rarely now.

There are brief moments when you delude yourself that you and Russell share the ultimate in intimate communication. Most of the time you feel more alone than you could ever have imagined possible. All that keeps you from suicide is the silly thought that Russell needs you, somehow, and there are days when it is a struggle to hold onto this idea. When you are in a black mood, being bitterly honest with yourself, you fear you are expendable, replaceable, and that if you disappear tomorrow, his life will go on without so much as a hiccup of sadness or regret. Annoyance, perhaps, that you have caused him to begin again the search for someone to take care of him. Excitement that the hunt can start anew and refresh him. There are days when you believe your life has absolutely no meaning.

You stare at the dead beings in these cases, thinking how fortunate they are. Their pain of living has been washed away by nothingness. How you envy them! You wonder what it feels like to die, if the soul exists as you once believed it does, if the spirit ascends. Or descends. The weight of hell's existence diminished once it became clear that you are already there.

Russell calls you to come look, and you join him before a case like the others, the case your shadow passed over. This one holds a girl, about your age. "This could be you," Russell says cheerfully. Her hair, or the tufts that remain, is the same color as your own, her eyes, the shape of her body. She is about as tall, and of similar weight. While not your twin, the resemblance is uncanny, enough to categorize you two as the same *type*. What is not the same is that her body is black, charred. "I couldn't tell you apart in a police lineup," Russell jokes. But you do not laugh. She is dead. You are alive. That he cannot appreciate a difference either means he is very sick, or that he sees little merit to you being alive or dead.

Looking into this case is too much like looking into a mirror. Her scorched features cannot disguise this: reflected back at you is an individual whose life was not under her control. A woman forced to a point of no return. She mirrors all of the qualities you loathe within yourself, and you are surprised when Russell reads her history to learn that she has committed atrocious acts. Acts that, on a bad day, reflect your most evil fantasies.

"'*Ann Marie Black.*' I'll say she's black! They burned her good. Pretty ordinary name," he says, as if her name disappoints him. As if he does not remember that your name is Marianne. You want to suggest he say her name backwards, but sense it will only lead to unpleasantness.

Ann Marie Black died on your birthday, three hundred

years before your birth. A remarkable coincidence you feel. Russell does not notice this, since he does not remember your birthday unless you remind him—you do not bring the coincidence to his attention. She died at the age you are now. You fantasize that as her soul departed her body it time-traveled, seeking through the centuries a new body, your body, and that your spirits are linked. Perhaps it is Ann Marie who dwells within you, who is sucking your vitality, causing you to subjugate your energy and stray from the path you were born to follow. Maybe this is why you feel such an eerie connection with the remains of this girl imprisoned in her case as you are imprisoned in your life.

You do not tell Russell your thoughts, of course, since from past experience you know he will be annoyed. At best he will call you silly. You cannot bear his disapproval.

Quickly he becomes tired of Ann Marie and moves away, down a corridor. He is bored with her as he becomes bored with you on a regular basis. You see him as a man who hides from his feelings, and from yours. He cannot be involved with the intricacies of true relationship. You know enough to realize that his boredom stems from an inability to allow your reality into his life. He is afraid that if he opens to you, he will lose himself—psychology 101. To disguise this, he pretends you are shallow. To protect him, you pretend to be so.

Right from the beginning you understood his fear, felt his pain. Back then, you struggled to express yourself to him, in a gentle and delicate way, to avoid intensifying his defenses. Then, on two occasions, your frustration grew. What escalated to shouting resulted in abandonment, and you had to work hard to bring him back to you. Now, you regret your actions, all of them. If he had simply drifted away then, perhaps your soul would belong to you still. But your love of Russell, your fear of losing him, his need of you, your naive idea that enough love would change him, all of it resulted in misguided actions that led to indenture. Slavery by its nature demands reassurance. But Russell's reaction has always been the same: he refuses to reassure you; he cuts you off before you can tell him what truly bothers you. You cannot recall when you stopped making the effort to confront him.

Now, he has no limits. He makes advances in your presence towards other women that you know he pursues when given a chance. You turn away from this disrespect, knowing but unknowing. You feel you have no options. You cannot tell him the hurt this behavior evokes in you, which you know he knows, since the one time long ago when you did discuss his infidelities, you made it clear. He has forgotten his vague statement that he would cease such activity, at least in your presence, which was the most you could hope for. Forgotten, or disregarded, since by now he knows he can do as he pleases. You are there for him, will always be there. Despite everything, you know he needs you and that need inspires your devotion. Love chains you to him, and your own need locks the chain in place. You despise yourself enough that no hate is left over for him.

You stare at this girl he has left you alone with. Her dead marble eyes seem to stare back. You expect her to move, to grin demonically, to show teeth like a vampire, her eyes to turn all white, her head to spin completely around. Nothing like this occurs, and this lack of movement is chilling because it seems too much like the non-reaction that has become your norm. No wonder Russell could not notice a difference. Her story begs to be re-read, and you stare at the plaque, letting the words that synopsize her life swirl through you. Your mind begins to run the video of her existence that you have produced from these words, and the script is all-too familiar. Her story is your story, the story of so many women over the world, over time, victims. Abuse that takes a variety of forms but culminates in annihilation.

Ann Marie is like a doll you played with as a child. You remember that doll vividly. Life-size, or your size. She walked and talked. Her verbal repertoire proved limited, but enough to create a dialogue. You wonder if Ann Marie will respond. You glance at the corridor Russell disappeared down—he is nowhere in sight.

"Hello!" you whisper. Your small voice, fragile as ash, drifts to you like a voice from another age that has managed to find an audio time machine.

Ann Marie says nothing. You stare at her face, willing her lips to move. And suddenly, to your half surprise, they do.

"Say again," you tell her, and press your ear to the glass case, waiting.

At the heart of darkness
blackness swirls
leeching light
pairing back time
sending you this message:
Your Shadow knows you well!

You are astonished. The poem you wrote, with your own hand, when you were young, with hopes, still studying, eager for life. A poem about the power of the shadowy self, the part of you that you do not know, perhaps do not care to know. No one read that poem, not even Russell—it is the only thing you have withheld from him.

"Did you say that?" you whisper.

You said that.

You stare at Ann Marie. Her cracked lips have moved again, you are certain. They now curl into a definite smile. She is a long-lost friend, a mother, a lover who sees you inside and out, who can touch your heart without inflicting pain. You are astonished at the realization of this perfection.

"She's a witch," a voice behind you says, and your body jerks. Russell stands so close. "She's got you talking to yourself. Maybe that's what you need, a doll. Someone to play with. A *playmate*." His grin is perverse.

Russell looks around. "There's nobody here," he says, and you know what he is thinking.

No! Don't let him!

"No, we can't——"

"Marianne, don't be selfish!" he tells you severely. But you are here, with him, and you will be an accessory.

No sooner has he said this than he orders, "Pick one."

"What?"

"There are plenty of bodies here. There's not even a guard. Nobody will miss it. Pick the one we take home."

A cold chill sucks at your blood, turning it to crimson glacial water that courses through your veins, cutting as it travels. "I just don't think——"

"Don't think. You're not good at it!" Russell laughs.

Choose another!

You stare at Ann Marie, helpless.

"Pick one, or I will."

You know that he wants you to pick Ann Marie. Clearly, he wants this one sitting on your couch upholstered with the flesh of an endangered species; joining you at the dining room table where the centerpiece is a bone he shoved into your purse at the catacombs; propped up on the toilet seat while you bathe; an arm draped languidly over the tombstone pilfered from a Boston cemetery; sleeping between you and Russell in your bed!

Horror causes you to tremble. This is the part of Russell that terrifies you. He has forced you yet again into a no-win situation. His is a win-win: If you love him, you will pick Ann Marie. If you do not love him, you will not choose, or you will choose another. And then you will be forced to deal with his displeasure which will result in rejection. All roads lead to the same place with Russell. Regardless of what you do, he will take Ann Marie.

Please, you think silently, hoping Ann Marie will hear you. And understand. There is no escape.

No!

"Her," you say, in a weak voice, your betraying finger shaking as you point.

"Give me your shoulder bag," he says, and you hand it over. This case, unlike the others, has no door, no lock. He uses the soft pigskin to try to smash the glass surrounding Ann Marie, but it will not yield.

I've warned you!

You mumble nervously, "Maybe we should forget——"

"Shut up!" Russell snaps, and glares at you. His eyes dart, rodent-like, around the room, searching for some implement that will destroy this barrier.

Don't do this!

He races down the corridor and quickly you lean into the glass to frantically whisper, "Please, please, forgive me. It will be okay. You'll be safe with me——"

As safe as you are?

The sweet voice has turned hard. You stare at Ann Marie and see that her smile has been replaced with a severe mouth. Her eyes accuse you.

She is right. You cannot defend yourself, let alone another. You step away from the glass.

"This should do it!" Russell says. He hefts the metal fire extinguisher and bashes it against the case. The glass quivers. He hits it harder. It spiderwebs.

Stop him!

Suddenly, he slams the metal through the glass. It shatters, sending shards everywhere, into his face, your arms, splattering blood over Ann Marie . . .

The scream rushes through a vortex of time. It is unbearable, and you cry out, clasping your hands over your ears as you back away.

The silence that follows is not complete. Your heart roars in your ears. Your body wants to convulse. You begin to retch.

Russell ignores you. He reaches into the case to grasp Ann Marie about the waist and lift her out. "She'll make a nice addition—What the—?" Suddenly, two scorched hands, more like claws, grasp his wrists. He is yanked forward. Into the case with her. On his knees.

"Fuck! Help! I'm stuck here. Something's caught me," he cries as he struggles with Ann Marie. You are shocked. Paralyzed. Encased in eternal time.

Russell's words finally penetrate beyond your ears, and your body moves forward instinctively. Your hands grab his waist to pull him out.

Your eyes lock with Ann Marie's. Red light flows from her to you and back again, the color of blood, a red river that spans the ages.

Go!

You understand. This will be your last chance, your only chance of freedom.

"Marianne, what the *fuck* are you doing! You're useless! Pull me out of here now!"

You release him. And step away. Back out of the room. Out the door which is not locked after all.

"Marianne, don't leave me! Please! Yes, go get help. But hurry back. Please!"

The words almost touch you. You hesitate only a moment, but then close the door on his demands. You have no intention of helping him anymore.

Immediately your eyes are drawn to the hot sunlight streaming from the sky. White light like fire, that burns away nightmares and memories and forms shadows. Shadows you no longer fear.

Ann Marie Black. A witch, the plaque said. Broiled alive in the sixteenth century. One of nine million killed over four centuries of the Inquisition. Because she was a woman? Living alone? Owning property? Her accusers insisted she cast spells, turned men into animals, evoked demons, brought evil into the world. She was all of that, but more. Her story is bigger, one you know intuitively. Of how strong women become weak. Of how they teach their daughters submission, silence and compliance as protection. Generation upon generation, living with a terror that mutates into something hideous and unnamable. You know Ann Marie's story well. It is a woman's story. Your story. And her revenge is your own. Your shadow, relaxed, stretches before you on the sidewalk, long and full, possessing a life of its own. "Hello, Ann Marie," you say, and hear her familiar voice answer back, "Hello!"

For the first time in a long time you smile; you do not feel alone. Then, suddenly, an old worry nags at you. "Russell's in good hands, isn't he? You'll take care of him, won't you?"

"Worry not!" A dark and powerful primordial voice like a shadow coming to life. "He is in our hands, but so are you!"

Your Essential Unsung Hero

Think about it: if the reel of existence had run out of film, would you be here talking with me now? Face it. You're here. I'm here. And you need me. Look, step into my screening room, where we can have some privacy and you can get a grip, okay?

By now you're wondering what movie is playing, right? Hell, you bought the ticket: Charon rowing the ancient Greeks across the river Styx; that sexy ethereal babe, the Angel of Death, seducing you into the arms of oblivion; old Jibrial greeting everybody at the tomb, at least the Muslims. It cracks me up, the way you people insist on a gender for your death images—we're working the lowest common denominator of scripting here—but at least decisions are being made. Gotta admit, though, the concept of Holy Ghost as Comforter nearly blew me away.

The funniest thing about you people is that you think in metaphor, so you gotta come up with the perfect character for your dissolution saga. It's kind of cute. Endearing. And I'm here to tell you, it's a good thing it's me you're meeting at the theater door. I speak your language, if you get the picture, and it helps that I'm pretty good with grease paint and special FX. I'll be whoever or whatever, your own personal Miracle Man or Invincible Woman of the nether world. Your biggest fantasy. Like I said, you need me.

Introductions? What's in a name? A guy comes by last week, about your age, a lot like you. Calls me, "Your Essential Unsung Hero." To be on the safe side, let's just leave it at that, okay?

So, what can I do for you? you ask. I mean, that's what everybody who passes this way asks. I think we should start at the beginning. By the time the final credits rolled, you were afraid. Alone. You needed help. You made promises you have no intention of keeping. Geez, you think I'm *meshuge?* Doesn't take a psychic to figure out you're desperate.

Look, basically I get you out of one place and, wham, into another. It's the *another* you're going ballistic about, right? You should. You don't know the half of it, believe me.

Let me race this by you: If you think it's all white light corridors shot through gauze and the ancestors pecking your cheek bones, you're dreaming. That's a come on. Clips that lure you into the dark theater. Then what? A nice long nap? Forget it! And you know it, too. I have yet to meet the person who truly believes he or she won't move on to some kind of sequel. Well, you got that right. Whether it's heaven, hell, purgatory, or another round on the old karmic wheel you're headed for, there's one thing you gotta remember, the thing you people always forget—you're taking yourself along.

What's that? You say you think you're gonna be somebody else? Who? Madonna with wings? Get real.

Now that you've got a grip, let me tell you where I flash into this picture. I'm not just some immortal who holds your sweaty hand through the scary bits. Think of me as a kind of movie critic for the newly departed. Sure, you could wander into the theater on your own. Maybe the worse that happens is you get stuck with the starring role in some grade Z porn, or appear in an endless loop of Edward D. Wood, Jr. films. But there's no shortage of soul-destroying stuff being produced. *Cinema of the Insane.* More than you bargained for. You could get hurt real bad. And, yes, there are things worse than death.

Of course, plenty of people deserve to go straight to hell, *Do Not Pass Go*, etc. You've said so yourself. At the moment, that might sound heartless, but it's not. I try to be fair, well, impartial anyway. But I kinda like you people, for the most part. You're so vulnerable when I see you. So open. Guts spilling out, sometimes literally. You bring out the nurturing me. And when you beg for help, like you just did, well, what am I supposed to do, keep paddling the damn canoe and pretend I'm deaf? Not in my nature, no matter what you imagine.

So, you've hit that place between features, when the lights go out. Questions? I've heard 'em all before: "Where am I?" "Where are you taking me?" "What's going to happen next?" This is where you *really* need me.

Okay, follow this script: First we go to the, well, think of it as the cutting room. You leave terra firma, you shed. I mean, we're talking spirit here. Soul. Between the cracks. A wrinkle in time and all that. It's not just the corporeal that's gotta be left behind, but all that other crap you lugged along—hopes; worries; regrets, blah, blah, blah. Chuck it at the door. For the next scene, it helps to be light and lean.

Now, here you are, standing in your naked subtle body, wondering what gives. You look at me. I look at you. You stare at the blank screen.

Suddenly you turn to me again, terrified of fate, and this is where it gets tricky. I know what you're about to project. And I can see in your spectral eyes you know too, even though you're avoiding it like the plague. Let me put it to you this way: if it's a good film, that's cool. The story will grab you, pull you in, and you won't demand a refund. But if you pick a turkey, for example, *Eternal Torment*, well . . . It's the uncut version, if you catch my drift.

My job description's simple: lead 'em out, take 'em to wherever they're headed. Straight forward. No overtime. If only I could just walk away! Maybe I've been at it too many millennia. Maybe I'm a primordial schmuck for letting myself bond with you people. All I know for sure is even the worst of you deserves a good show. That's why you need me. I see advance screenings, so I know what tortures and pleasures you're capable of inflicting on yourself. It's the worst of you picks the worst movies. Why? *Method Acting 101.* If you'd felt good about yourself, you'd have gotten lost in a story crammed with possibilities, and you'd have invited all your friends along for the ride. But your taste was off kilter. Maybe way off. So you picked a rotten film. For you. For everybody you dragged along. And here you are, before the eternal projector, ready to crank out yet another visual monstrosity.

So, what do I know that you don't? Bottom line: there's more than one film available. Maybe two, maybe seven. Maybe twenty thousand. And the cans are filled with all that you can imagine—Virgin-Whore, God-Devil, Nirvana-Oblivion—and every shade between. The point is, people like you can't see that because you didn't think you'd have a choice. You don't expect it here because most of you didn't know you had choices back there.

Look, I know all this is confusing, and you might not appreciate it at the moment, but I'm risking a lot by helping you, so we've got to cut to the chase. You don't have a clue what bizarre energies scuttle through the universe. I mean, you people make statues of Kali with her eight flailing arms. Right! You should see the real thing. And those paintings of a horned Satan in a red bodysuit. Let's just say he and I have had a few run-ins. He is one mean s.o.b., but don't quote me. You don't have to hang out with them, I do. Hidden agendas abound and in my circle interference is frowned upon. You folks are supposed to have free will and all, that's the plan. And you do. It's just that the censors got to you and now you've convinced yourself you don't have a choice, and that doesn't sit right with me.

I can see you're nervous. Afraid of getting yourself into a situation. Fortunately, there's the unexpected. Me. Instead of sitting on my thumbs, I'm about to perform a miracle. Think of me as a blue-ray player, technology personified. But instead of entire films, I show nothing but trailers. Not the movies you've *seen*, the ones you *could see*, if you only you wanted to. All you have to do is gaze into my eyes. Trust me. The rest, my friend, will someday be history. Yours.

Well, you look a hell of a lot better than when you arrived. Hop in the boat and I'll give you a lift. Oh, just one more thing. If word gets out I'm, you know, helping people . . . Yikes! I don't even want to think about it. Let's just say I've got a lot of concerns here, not the least of which is that all the good jobs are taken. Being bored for eternity sucks. And to tell the truth, I'd be pretty lonely without humanoids like you to usher through the beyond. You make my day, infinitely speaking.

So, next time my name, whatever it is to you, comes up in conversation, keep it simple, stupid. Everything I've said is between you, me and the cosmic popcorn machine. Trust me, it's better this way. I'll do filmic damage control, but you gotta keep our little secret. If anybody asks, you decided all by yourself. A hero from where? Saved from the jaws of what?

You've been watching too many movies.

Acknowledgments

"Always a Castle?" First published in *Gothic Lovecraft,* ed. S. T. Joshi & Jason Brock (Cycatix Press, 2016); reprinted in *Lovecraft Mythos* (Flame Tree Press, 2020).

"Cold Comfort." Original to this collection.

"A Crazy Mistake," first published in *The Madness of Cthulhu 2,* ed. S. T. Joshi (Titan Books, 2015).

"Death Dreaming," first published in *Nightmare's Realm,* ed. S. T. Joshi (Dark Regions Press, 2017).

"Eye of the Beholder," first published in *Dreams of the Witch House,* ed. Lynne Jamneck (Dark Regions Press, 2016).

"Flesh and Bones," first published in *Searchers After Horror: New Tales of the Weird and Fantastic,* ed. S. T. Joshi (Fedogan & Bremer, 2014).

"Gurrl UnDeleted," first published in *Dark Fusions,* ed. Lois Gresh (PS Publishing, 2013).

"Mourning People," first published in *Innsmouth Nightmares,* ed. Lois H. Gresh (PS Publishing, 2015).

"The Oldies," first published in *Black Wings V,* ed. S. T. Joshi (PS Publishing, 2016; Titan Books, 2017).

"Sympathy for the Devil," first published in *Chilling Tales,* ed. Michael Kelly (Edge SF & F Publishing, 2011).

"Trogs," first published in *Apostles of the Weird,* ed. S. T. Joshi (PS Publishing, 2020).

"The Visitor," first published in *Black Wings VI,* ed. S. T. Joshi (PS Publishing, 2017; Titan Books, 2018).

"Your Essential Unsung Hero," first published in *Xanadu 3,* ed. Jane Yolen (TOR Books, 1995).

"Your Shadow Knows You Well," first published in *Dark Terrors 6: The Gollancz Book of Horror,* ed. Stephen Jones and David Sutton (Orion Press/Gollancz 2002).

Made in the USA
Middletown, DE
23 October 2023

41276871R00116